garden

JUNK

garden JUNK

Mary Randolph Carter

Photographs by the Author

Design by
Tracy Monahan

PENGUIN
STUDIO

PENGUIN STUDIO
Published by the Penguin Group
Penguin Putnam Inc., 375 Hudson Street,
New York, New York 10014, U.S.A.
Penguin Books Ltd, 27 Wrights Lane,
London W8 5TZ, England
Penguin Books Australia Ltd, Ringwood,
Victoria, Australia
Penguin Books Canada Ltd, 10 Alcorn Avenue,
Toronto, Ontario, Canada M4V 3B2
Penguin Books (N.Z.) Ltd, 182–190 Wairau Road,
Auckland 10, New Zealand

Penguin Books Ltd, Registered Offices:
Harmondsworth, Middlesex, England

First published in 1997 by Penguin Studio,
a member of Penguin Putnam Inc.

1 3 5 7 9 10 8 6 4 2

Grateful acknowledgment is made for permission to reprint
an excerpt from *Travels with Charley* by John Steinbeck.
Copyright © The Curtis Publishing Co., 1961, 1962.
Copyright © John Steinbeck, 1962.
Copyright renewed Elaine Steinbeck, Thom Steinbeck
and John Steinbeck IV, 1989, 1990. Used by permission of
Viking Penguin, a division of Penguin Books USA Inc.

CIP data available

Printed in Singapore
ISBN 0-670-86938-4

To my mother—
you stole my heart
in your herb garden.

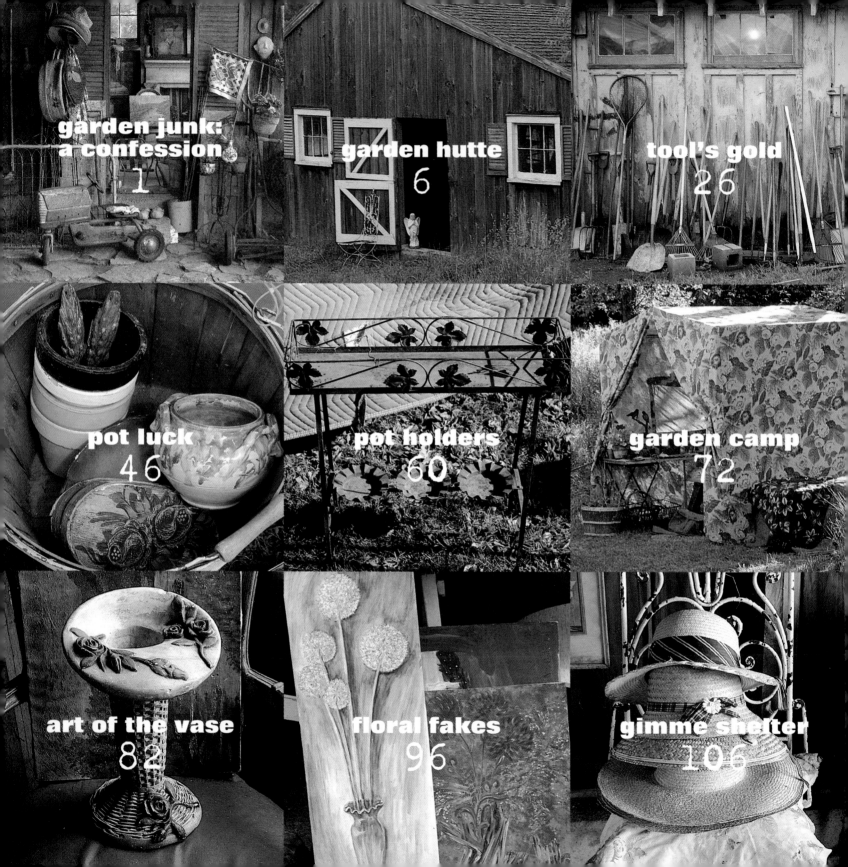

acknowledgments

Growing a book is a little like growing a garden. You need good soil, a receptive climate, diligent weeders, watchful waterers, and generous praise when the peonies bloom—and the roses don't! My family has provided the soil, the fair skies, the weeders, the waterers. They are the loyal scarecrows, the wakeful guardians, the daring keepers of my garden heart—weeds, junk, and all.

Homage to a Matisse tea party, by my brother, Jimmie.

Mother and Father, what a garden you have nurtured—Cary, Nell, Jimmie, Emily, Liza, Bernard, Christian, Cleiland, and me! It grows and grows to include all of our families—thirty-three now! With Sister and Jean—whoops, now thirty-five! Thank you, family. And merci beaucoup, Jimmie, for your wonderful Matisse interpretation (seen at left), and Cary for my portrait, and Cleiland for catching me in the fields of junk!

Twenty-six years of stopping, starting, turning the car around for a fleeting scrap of something on the side of the road that called "treasure" only to me, only for me. You weeded, you sowed, you mowed, mowed, mowed. Thank you always, Howard.

Carter, you have seen the light of junking! You are my happiest convert. The Garden Hutte is as much your invention as mine. Thank you for your hauling, digging, planting, growing.

Sam, you have not succumbed, but your independence allows for mine. Thank you, but wait a minute—what about that old trunk, the peeling sign, the vintage van Gogh you hauled back to Hobart? Are you coming around, Sam? I can wait.

Thank you Ralph. It's been almost a decade since we sat among your collected treasures in your scrapbook office and you welcomed me into your Polo family. Your inspiration is always personal, and honest—filled with romance, optimism, and your own special laughter. Thank you Buffy, my Polo soul-sister and this year garden sister. Thanks for the baskets, dead topiaries, garden tools, pots, and your wheelbarrow (still safe in my Garden Hutte), and particularly for all the ripe bags of manure! And thank you to the rest of my Polo family, especially Kerry Irvine, my seventh sister (for so-oooo much!), Pat Christman, Deborah Schacht, Michael Morelli, Renee Wightman, and Susan Stevens. And a big thank you to the whole Polo Advertising Department for my garden junk birthday and my very own office tractor!

Thank you, Ellen O'Neill (how many times can I delight in your junk?), and Doug Bihlmaier for the junking leads in Colorado. Thank you, Mark Campbell and Didier Malige for all the junk collaborations. Thank you Gret Warren, the wizard-creator of my garden tent. And a special thanks to Bruce Weber for inspiring my Room with a View, and so much more!

Thank you, good friends Sam and Gloria Landers, Kim Rockefeller, Riki and Bob Larimer, Aaron and Judy Daniels, Joel and Rhona Bross, Peter and Joan Diamandis, Helen Spector, Robert Carter Ball, Marie-France Boyer, Marcia Weinberg Mossack, and Brigitte Lacombe.

Thank you, junking friends and gardeners in the North Country—Joe Zullo and Bobby, Helen and Alexander Hutchinson, Kevin de Martine, Laurie Higgins, Maureen Rodgers, Maurice Neville, Jerry Winrow, Lisa Durfee, Karen Murphy, Kitty Paris, Josh Paris, Bettina Calderone, Alice Reid, and Mike Fallon, his family, and helpers.

Thank you, kindred junkers north, south, east, and west! On the Outer Banks—Charles Reber, Jerry Pontes, Karen Sawin, Jo Ruth Patterson, and the Bermuda Triangle gang! Stephanie Morgan-Rogers in Colorado; Judy Shoup and Phyllis Schuster in Florida; Ben Apfelbaum and Holly Graham in Atlanta; John Halpern, Joanne Zolner, Antonia Goodspeed, Lora Zarubin, Honey Wolters, Sharone Einhorn, and Rebecca Cole in New York; Paul Forsyth in Houston; Beverly Daniloff, and Laurie, Eddie, and Samantha Warner-Garrick in Los Angeles; Pat Lawson Kyzer and Rebecca Silberman in Virginia, and Judy McGowan in Chicago.

Special thanks to my new friends/new team—my wordsmith-poet editor Sarah Scheffel, and master craftswoman art director Tracy Monahan. What a beginning—late nights, Saturdays and Sundays, messengers, messages, faxes, good faith, good humor, and endless laughter for the book that wouldn't end. (It's just the beginning!) Thank you Laura Healy for following up on all my junker's hot spots, and Roni Axelrod, production director extraordinaire! As always, a big hug and many thanks to Michael Fragnito, my publisher: You planted a beanstalk for me at Viking (now Penguin) Studio four books and nine years ago! I'm still climbing, don't let go! Thank you, Steve Axelrod, my agent who picks me up, spurs me on, and really does seem to see what I see.

Finally, a very special thank you to the neighborly guardians and gardeners of the Garden Hutte—Elsie and Bob Albig. And to all those who plant, water, weed, and believe that spring will really come, and a great garden junk treasure is right around the corner.

If I seem to be over-interested in junk, it is because I am, and I have a lot of it, too—half a garage full of bits and broken pieces. I use these things for repairing other things. Recently I stopped my car in front of the display yard of a junk dealer near Sag Harbor. As I was looking courteously at the stock, it suddenly occurred to me that I had more than he had. But it can be seen that I do have a genuine and almost miserly interest in worthless objects. My excuse is that in this era of planned obsolescence, when a thing breaks down I can usually find something in my collection to repair it—a toilet, or a motor, or a lawn mower. But I guess the truth is that I simply like junk.

John Steinbeck,
Travels with Charley

garden junk: a confession

If there were a lie-detector test for a gardener, I would probably fail. As children we were always poking buttercups under each other's chins to see if we liked butter—I think a gardener's test should be just as romantic. I picture myself hooked up to a large sunflower by wiry grape and honeysuckle vines. "How many bulbs did you plant last fall?" "What is the highest mountain of weeds you ever pulled?" "Is a leek an allium?" "Would you name your firstborn after Gertrude Jekyll?" Except for the Gertrude Jekyll question, I would certainly have failed. I am <u>not</u> a gardener, just a devoted aspirant.

All my life I have loved creating environments with found things, arranging and putting them together indoors. (When you live in a city apartment with only a view of trees and earth, you have few choices!) With the purchase of Elm Glen Farm eight years ago (more about that on page 9), my options changed. My old passion for collecting and arranging moved outdoors. Before the garden was ever planned I began the hunt for its furnishings—old, peeling lawn chairs and tables, tools, fences, wagons, barrows, gates, bird baths, trellises, vases, crocks, pots, and pot holders—even a toy tractor. My inspiration came from van Gogh's sunflowers, Bonnard's still lifes, Matisse's painted vases, and Monet's gardens. My search began in other people's yards and garages, flea markets, junk shops, salvage jungles, and side-of-the-road giveaways!

A decade ago when I visited Sissinghurst, the home of the English writer and gardener Vita Sackville-West, I was much more inspired by the <u>paintings</u> of flowers tucked away in her writing tower, and her little stone garden bench with an upholstered seat of herbs, than with all those glorious beds of roses. I approach gardening with a collector's heart. First things first: the bed, <u>then</u> the roses!

Left: At the entrance of the Garden Hutte, the heart of my garden paradise at Elm Glen Farm, an exhibition of gardening junk—from a garden gate to a potty flowerpot stand—foraged from far and wide. A rusty but reliable push-mower centurion guards it all.

Above: My home-crafted signpost pointing to the garden junking landscapes to be tilled in the pages to come. Dig in!

Since the publication of *American Junk* in 1994, I've discovered that I am <u>not</u> alone in my belief in the worth of the worthless, the usefulness of the used, and the exhilaration of the hunt for the impossibly-wonderful-something. "Nothing can relate my feelings for rummaging through piles and piles of stuff looking for treasures," Paul Forsyth wrote from Houston, Texas. Joanne Zolner from Niswkayuna, New York, confessed, "I have been a scavenger ever since the seventies...so it was great to give my hobby some validation...." Antonia Sonspeed, from Putnam Valley, New York, described herself and a junking friend as "unrepentant collectors." <u>Oh, aren't we all?!</u> Whether it's a flea market of three hundred dealers, a five-family garage sale, or one chock-full little side-of-the-road table—I am <u>equally</u> inspired and heart-thumpingly thrilled. I <u>know</u> there is something out there that I can't live without!

1. The What-Cha-Ma-Call-It Store in upstate New York, filled with the abandoned goods of our daily lives, is an icon for junk shops all over America.

4. Flea markets like the Elephant's Trunk in New Milford, Connecticut (and all those listed in the Junk Guide, pages 228–39), are permanently scheduled every weekend or once a month. It's good to know there are resources you can count on.
5. As a reformed antiquer, now die-hard junker, I would normally pass up a shop that has an "Antiques" sign displayed so prominently. Don't be a snob—you never know what you might find among all that inviting stuff beckoning to you through the window.

2. & 3. Two ways to junk, at top in the fresh air at an outdoor flea market, garage, yard or tag sale, or above, indoors in a real shop, like Madalin in Tivoli, New York. Both options offer creative pickings served up in a delicious potluck style.

6. The Amenia Auction Gallery, Amenia, New York, used to be a church. My favorite junk outpost in Millerton, New York, the Rummage Shoppe, was a muffler shop in the fifties. Junking is not just for the junk. Enjoy exploring the unusual recycled spaces you'll discover it in!

13. Classic gardening books, like *The Gardener's Catalogue*, are yet another treasure to be reaped along the garden junking trail.

7. Very often, usually on holiday weekends, shops will spill their goods out onto the front lawn, transforming it into a tempting yard sale.
8. Streamline the hunt by focusing on a category like Garden Junk, then pots, and unearth a jewel-encrusted one-of-a-kind.

9. In your quest for Garden Junk, don't exclude flower shows and nurseries. This blooming fellow was the welcoming committee at a Richmond, Virginia, flower show. A nice idea, too, as a fanciful character (scarecrow?) in your garden, and a good way to put some of those clay pots to use!

10 & 11. Gardeners, throw down your trowels and spades, and head for a day of digging in the fertile fields of junk. Be on the lookout for artful vases to show off your prized peonies.
12. You won't find Klutter Korner in Dunedin, Florida, listed in a guide to antiquing. You have to know a friend-in-the-know (like I did) or keep your eyes peeled as you travel those backroads.

junk journals

It started during my Beauty Editor days at *Mademoiselle* magazine. On every shoot I would tape in a Polaroid shot of the model and swatch in samples of her makeup so that we could identify every product. I had always been a diarist—doing it as part of my job was even better.

When I began junking, I carried my Polaroid tucked into a little army surplus pouch, seen slung around my neck at right. I'd capture my treasure at the place it was discovered. (Not unlike those newborn baby pics snapped in the hospital moments after the birth.) Along with the pic taped in my junk journal went the price, the dealer's card, the receipt, and anything special about the piece I wanted to remember. For *Garden Junk* I filled about six volumes (see two below), and the spirit of them is in the Junk Guide.

My notebook of choice is an 8-inch by 10-inch spiral-bound sketch book. (I hoard the stock from my country drugstore.) Decorate each cover with something akin to what's inside—e.g., the china fruit cornucopia on the cover below, a Xerox blowup of the original, graces volume IV, featuring fruits and veggies junk.

transport

Never let your booty become a burden as you're on the prowl. Most flea market dealers are more than happy to let you store your wares at their site until you've finished your tour of duty. The trick is to remember the drop-off spots. Make mental notes, since most don't have names and can look alike.

Another boost is a shopping cart or a little wagon (like the one I'm towing in the picture at top, which was actually a purchase, not a think-ahead strategy!). Some flea markets, like the Elephant's Trunk in New Milford, Connecticut, supply carts, as seen above.

be prepared

I have found a fisherman's vest with many pockets to be the essential junking wardrobe must-have. Each pocket, clockwise from top left, organizes a junk hunt tool.

- Sun Lotion: SPF, your choice. A Swiss Army knife—the little scissors are indispensable.
- Wash'n Dri towelettes: It's dirty out there, and so is the stuff you'll be handling. Though you may be lucky enough to find a toilet, you'll rarely find a sink. And speaking of toilets, carry a small pack of tissues.
- Cash and checks: There's a lot out there for a dollar or two. Take along twenty singles, and a few fives or tens. Some people don't like to make change, or don't have it, plus cash can often make you a better deal. I always carry a couple of checks for bigger purchases. Most dealers accept them—just bring proper identification.
- A list: Writing it all down will keep you focused. Can you stray from the list? Junking is about straying. This is your lifeline when you need it.
- A disposable camera: To record your treasures. If you prefer a Polaroid camera, you'll need a larger pocket or a pouch. Mine (see top left) is army surplus.

big deals

Junking is about dealing. Standard question: "Can you do any better?" Dealers expect the question, and usually can. Don't ask an individual price. Wait until you've gathered together everything you're interested in, then ask. If the items are 50 cents like the gloves at left, I'd plop down two quarters and run.

junkers m.o.

When I hit an establishment or flea market, no matter how large or small, my M.O. (modus operandi) is the same. Case the place before making a purchase. (This is admittedly hard, if not virtually impossible, at a really huge market, but still I try.) Junker's caveat: If you see something you really love, and it seems like a pretty good deal, don't walk away...unless you're prepared to lose it. I have!

junk drivers

If you do drive and junk be aware of normal drivers on the road—particularly those behind you. If you see something that appears to be a roadside pull-over possibility, no jamming on the brakes. Pull over and take a look. I try to warn other drivers to beware of me—with my "I Brake for Junk" bumper sticker. Information on how to order one under American Junk Journal, page 239.

dress code

- My friend and artist Kerry Irvine painted flowers, fruits, and vegetables on a pair of comfy overalls for my garden junking expeditions. Comfort is the rule. Be prepared to peel. Dress in light layers.
- Shade your face. Protect your head. Baseball caps or fishing caps are standard fare. I'm hooked on an old captain's cap. It's cotton, cool, and very light (see me in it, opposite page).
- Sunglasses, if you like, but make sure they're secured in some way—with a croakie or string. There's a lot of putting on and taking off during inspections.
- Rain in the forecast? Fold up a poncho (there are really tiny ones that will fit in your vest pocket).
- Happy feet, happy junker. Choose comfortable footwear that can withstand dust, mud, and long hours of standing. I opt for old, really worn-in, laceless sneakers.

garden hutte

Carl Larsson, *The Cottage*, 1894-97, The National Museum in Stockholm

t was a Swedish love story set in a Scandinavian artist colony in the French farm village of Grez-sur-Loing just south of Paris. Carl Larsson and Karin Bergöö met there, and were married in Sweden in 1883. Three years later they were given the little cottage by the creek, known as Lilla (Little) Hyttnäs. Situated in the village of Sundborn in central Sweden, it reminded them of their farmhouse in Grez. In 1901, after summers of work, Carl and Karin and their seven children moved in full-time. For over two decades it was not only their home but a living canvas for their collective talents and the backdrop for Carl's hundreds of watercolors celebrating his family's life. *The Cottage*, seen above, an early watercolor of Little Hyttnäs, was what I envisioned when I first saw the softly weathered red barn of Elm Glen Farm, seen at left. We bought it in the summer of 1988, and seven summers later its transformation began. The Garden Hutte, seen on the preceding pages and the next sixteen, is my Little Hyttnäs filled with the spirit of all its special inhabitants—Carl, Karin, Suzanne, Ulf, Pontus, Lisbeth, Brita, Kersti, and baby Esbjorn. Welcome.

Above: *The Cottage*, a watercolor view of Little Hyttnäs from the Sundborn River as seen by Carl Larsson around 1894.
Left: My view of the barn at Elm Glen Farm snapped with a Polaroid camera. The low shed attached to the right of the main structure was resurrected along with a garage (not shown), to its right, and transformed into my Garden Hutte.
Preceding pages: Of all the views of the Garden Hutte, this is my favorite. I love the way the roofline reaches down to the little row of white-trimmed windows. Two of the three on the left side were newly cut in, as was the Dutch door with its welcoming angel. The day I took this picture, June 11, 1995, I wrote in my journal, "My dream of Carl Larsson's cottage comes to realization."

1.

2.

3.

4.

5.

1. The angel of the Garden Hutte ($25, from Stan'z Used Items & Antiques, Kingston, New York) arrived at Elm Glen Farm, rolled out of the back of the car, and broke into two concrete chunks. A bad omen thwarted by a good layer of cement glue. **2.** A painting by Jack Baretto, the former owner, of the barn in 1955. **3.** As shown in this photograph taken in the summer of 1995, not too much has changed except the weathered-down paint and the replacement of three-quarters of the garage door with windows. **4 & 5.** These two small pictures tell the story of the transformation of the shed from January to August. The full story just ahead!

2.

1.

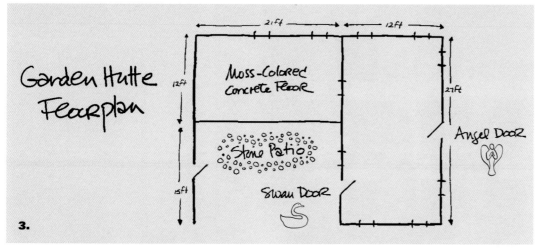

Garden Hutte
Fearplan

21ft
12ft

Moss-Colored
Concrete Floor

12ft

27Ft

Stone Patio

Angel Door

Swan Door

15ft

3.

4.

5.

Though I yearned for a garden at Elm Glen Farm, I must admit it was a home for all of that glorious garden junk that I yearned for most. A garden would legitimize my appetite for yet another romantic, slightly dilapidated—and this time mossy (!)—retreat. I would fill it with every conceivable kind of garden tribute—from venerably rusty clippers to outrageously ornamental vases, tumbling stacks of clay pots, gardening stands, peeling yard furniture, flower paintings, baskets, floppy straw hats, garden sculpture, carts and wagons, whimsical birds, mysterious elves, and an angel at my door.

Counterclockwise: 1. A winter view of the barn garage annex from the west before the door was cut in, before the shutters and trellis were added, and before the Garden Hutte angel took her post as seen the following fall, at top left. **3.** A floorplan of the Garden Hutte and shed, designating the two entrances into the Hutte—the "swan" door from under the shed and the "angel" door from the west. **4.** A view of the Garden Hutte after three-quarters of the old garage door was replaced by windows. The lower quarter of the door, left intact, can be seen under the green window boxes. **5.** The view from the Garden Hutte windows before the fence, seen in 4, was built.

Above: The picture above illustrates my plight! The shed outside what is now the Hutte had protected horses from unpleasant weather. When the horses left, our junk pile took over. Luckily I was introduced to Maurice Neville, a junkman extraordinaire, who in a couple of hours filled (no—crammed!) the back of his truck with the detritus of our first five years at Elm Glen Farm and hauled it off. Away with the old basketball hoop, the rusted-out barbecue grill, the metal kitchen cabinet, the shutters—"Oh no! not the shutters," and the old trellis, a relic of a garden that bloomed at Elm Glen before our arrival. My one regret—the old string clothes dryer hanging on the wall to the right of the trellis. It would have made a fantastic plant hanger!

Left: The only thing blooming outside the "swan" entrance to my Garden Hutte appears to be the geraniums perched on the trellis. Of course, they don't count, being artist-grown. The four little dried-out moss trees below it aren't valid, and certainly not the topiary skeleton perched between the swan and the shuttered door! A glimpse of sunflowers glowing from a pillow just inside (more about it on page 145) gives us a glimmer of hope. And through the Palladian window—found at Stan'z Used Items & Antiques, king of salvage, in Kingston, New York, for $75, and cut into the previously blank wall by master carpenter Joseph Zullo—there is a vase of pastel poppies and a flowered urn (more on both on page 113). "Objection! They fall into the same category as the geranium painting." Do topsy-turvy pots, waiting to be stuffed with moist earth and fledgling plants score points? And, what about a warhorse of a watering can, resting at far left in the hollow of a seatless stool, waiting to nourish them? Even the swan, a leftover parade float decoration, looks a little parched. A word in my defense—it was early spring, and even the forsythia hadn't bloomed!

Though I've long been on the witness stand defending why there is no living bloom outside this entrance to my Garden Hutte, seen at right and on the preceding pages, let me state it a little more clearly. Nothing could bloom in a place like this that is totally covered. What's at work here is garden sleight of hand: the illusion of a garden that will never require sunshine or rain. Herewith, a roadmap to this chorus line of everlasting garden paraphernalia. The total cost came in at around $179, the most expensive item being the window for $75.

An instant forest of moss-covered topiaries—four for $20—baking outside Cindy's Antiques, Amenia, New York, has found a cooler home on a $15 plant stand resuscitated with dark green enamel. (More on rusty recoveries, page 174.)

Even Mike Fallon, the owner and chief auctioneer of Copake Country Auction, Copake, New York, scratched his head when I had to have this pair of topiary frames. They reminded me of a more primitive version of those in the Queen's rose garden in *Alice in Wonderland*. The pair was $40.

Every weekend we pass a giant swan—once a parade float decoration—that now towers over its owner's two-story home. (It gives me pleasure to know there are collectors crazier than I!) My little swan made of chicken wire covered with a sort of sandpaper reminds me of an elegant garden sculpture.

Waiting for a ride home, the group below (a seed spreader for $5, a watering can for $20, and an ash can—a junker's "gift with purchase") was scavenged at Stan'z Used Items & Antiques, Kingston, New York. To the left, a watering can tilting in a seatless stool ($2, Amenia Auction Gallery, Amenia, New York) and an ash can propped on a stool ($5 from Bottle Shop Antiques, Washington Hollow, New York) create a kind of garden symmetry.

I like to think that the <u>grand</u> trellis (above), as I call it, left behind by Helen Hutchinson, the former owner of Elm Glen Farm and a dedicated gardener, was perhaps meant as a kind of garden-warming present for us. Today it remains not far from where I originally found it, and serves as a <u>grand</u> perch for another present—the still life of geraniums, last year's Christmas gift from Didier Malige. The windows, by the way, seen at far left next to the trellis, were left behind too. We've used them to replace the garage door of the Garden Hutte, creating the view seen on page 11.

The garden Hutte

Above: In villages like Sundborn in Sweden where Karin and Carl Larsson created their perfect home, it is the custom to paint a welcoming message above the door. The day I painted "The Garden Hutte" on my door, I pinned a miniature tin butterfly above it (a gift from my sister Liza). My son Carter hung a little bouquet he had just picked from the field.

It's the strangest thing, but when I placed the two sets of old green-blue shutters (seen at right) on either side of the Garden Hutte entrance, I was dreaming of those tall, stately Buckingham Palace Guards with their skyscraper black helmets. I used to be accused (mostly by my husband, Howard) of an addiction to homeless and hapless chairs. Add to that a hopeless love for old shutters—the more weathered, the more peeling and flaking, the better. Look around—you will see them. Little leaning stacks of them in the barn, in the carriage house in the woodshed. When the Garden Hutte creation began, they were already there, ready to take their places at the doorway and at each window. Every shutter found a home, so for the moment I am exonerated!

 # don't shutter
(tips on fix-ups)

Drive into almost any junk or salvage yard and you're welcomed by armies of shutters. No lack of them means bargains. I've never paid more than several dollars for one, and recently I picked up the group seen below right for nothing! (They were put out with the trash on the side of our country road!)

The toughest time I've had in shutter sleuthing was to come up with three pairs all the same size to camouflage a stretch of new (ugly!) windows put into our city bedroom. Best tip: Write window measurements down and stick them in your wallet. You never know when you'll see that stack on the side of the road. If it's a nonspecific hunt, I always go for the tall ones. You can cut them down to size, which is exactly what we did for the little windows of the Hutte. Joe Zullo, my construction adviser, placed them across his sawhorses (seen at top left) and zipped them in half with his skilsaw. See the results below left, and a fuller view on page 11, top left.

I love the mottled, weathered colors of old shutters. If you don't— deflake with a sturdy wire brush or steel wool, hit with a hose, air-dry, and spray-paint.

Top: My lucky day at a Memorial Day sale at Copake Country Auction grounds in Copake, New York. For $200, I took home everything piled up under the tree—over sixty items! The find of the day was the portrait (a reproduction, of course) of Armand Roulin by Vincent van Gogh, seen in the lower left corner, and again at left in its place of honor in the Garden Hutte.

Above left: The mantelpiece, $60 at Stan'z Used Items & Antiques in Kingston, New York, awaits transfer to its new home, at left. The wire chair looking a lot like a proud peacock was $10 less, also from Stan'z, and is seen again on the following page.

Above right: A pair of scroll-backed metal garden chairs, $100 from (where else?) Stan'z. See one at far left.

Left: The eastern wall of the Garden Hutte, punctuated by a high window and the angel's door, is lined from left to right with a pair of pastel-colored still lifes—more booty from the pile under the tree at Copake (seen at top). Below them, paint-by-number ballerinas and a still life of lilies, both $1, from Stan'z. The white scrolled-back metal chair (*sans* a seat) is revisited on page 182. The little red round table top propped on a blue metal stand was a $5 put-together also from Stan'z. The Louis XV chair was recycled as an easel for a primitive landscape—both hauled away from a hot dusty field near Hillsdale, New York, $20 and $5 respectively. The fossilized ivy topiaries tucked under the mantel saw better days with my friend Buffy Birrittella.

Above: The attraction to my stairway to nowhere, reclaimed at a Copake Country Auction years ago for $10, was the pink paint fading on the sides. It is now booby-trapped (see opposite page for a front-on view) with pruning shears and pots so no one can climb near the fair hatted gardener at the top. She and her sister, to the right of her, were the two prizes discovered at Bottle Shop Antiques in Washington Hollow, New York, for $50.

Right: The western wall of the Garden Hutte, opposite that on the preceding pages, starts with a portrait of a lady with a commanding straw hat and peonies, pulled from a stack at Cindy's Antiques, Amenia, New York, for $40. She anchors other floral works, bookended by two amazing Palladian windows (I couldn't contain my ecstasy—not a great way to bargain—when I first saw them), $75 each at Stan'z, Kingston, New York. Dangling near the storage steps at far right is an odd assortment of rusty clippers. Rejuvenating them is an option (see page 31), or think of them as the cutting edge of wall decor! The child's toy wheelbarrow, set like a rusty sculpture on the mustard-colored table, was $5 at a Copake tag sale (more on wheel things on page 154). The small framed painting squeezed next to the window, at the far right, is my jewel in the crown. I <u>love</u> that little lady in the flowered dress and perky straw hat! I clutched it to my heart at a local tag sale, paid my 50 cents, and called it a perfect day.

Right: Like every gardener, I collect scraps of garden inspiration—postcard replicas of O'Keeffes, Hockneys, Bonnards, Carl Larsson watercolors, seed packages, fantasy gardens torn from magazines, Polaroids of favorite gardeners and some of my own prizes! The problem is always where to display them so the dream is not lost or trashed! My gardener's chicken-wire bulletin board tacked onto the back of the Garden Hutte door has renewed my hope and my collecting.

Opposite page: Pinned, tucked, and wedged behind a chicken-wire frame are, clockwise from the top left, a souvenir seed package of a sunflower favorite, an embroidered geranium coaster, a carload of giant blackberries, a dried sunflower pointing to *The Terrace at Vernon*, by Pierre Bonnard, overlapping a huge watermelon, and to the left of the Bonnard, *Mount Fuji*, painted by David Hockney after a visit to Japan.

the gardener's bulletin board

I was poking around in the lower level of the barn attached to the Garden Hutte by an open shed when I spied an old bale of chicken wire neatly tied up. I had been thinking about how to create a gardener's bulletin board to decorate the back of the Hutte door (it's just a forlorn piece of plywood), so I knew I'd found my solution. In less than ten minutes, the wire was cut and stapled into place. I used the wire openings to secure my garden treasures. A staple makes a good stabilizer to prop a card on, and stick pins are good insurance to keep cards from sliding around. Tuck cards under the wire and pin or tie objects on top. Dried flowers, an old garden glove, a toy trowel can add dimension and fun!

Top left and right: At least eight years had passed since a horse had made a home under the shade of the Garden Hutte shed. But before this, many had. The 21 by 27-foot area was sloped unevenly from the back to the front, and was lumpy from a million rocks (boulders some), dirt, and layers (and layers!) of dried manure. Like a mad archaeologist on a dig, I got to know all of these layers down-on-my-knees intimately! After decorating my Hutte, I had this vision (yes, another one) of a primitive kind of shaded patio under the attached shed looking out at (and over!) my new fence (see opposite page) to the mountains and the gardens to come. The back half would be paved with something sturdy. (Ultimately, I chose cement. Check the end result on pages 186–87.) My son Carter helped with the front half. It was backbreaking, like doing a giant jigsaw puzzle with three- and four-pound stones. Most people have the land leveled and rolled. I dug, raked, and leveled the best I could, then laid the thin (2-inch), uneven wall stones—a pallet of them. After the stones were placed, I spread stone dust between the crevices and watered it all down. The floor flip-flops a little when you walk on it, but time and the elements will steady it.

1. The crate of stone dust, $32 a yard, is forklifted over the Garden Hutte. 2. Carter places a large piece of plastic in the yard to catch it. We ordered much too much stone dust, and ended up with a mountain of it that made a huge mess. I decided I don't like stone dust and would have been just as happy with sand or dirt. 3. The stone dust is emptied onto the plastic. Try to contain it as best you can. Don't over order. I needed only three-quarters of a yard. 4. The pallet of uneven thin wall stone cost $200. It covered approximately half of the earthen floor. I bought it at Ed Herrington, Inc., a huge lumber, mill work, and building materials place in Hillsdale, New York. They deliver and unload at no extra cost. 5. The stones are beautiful, but very heavy. Protect your hands with heavy gloves. Carter lugged them into the shed, where I would painstakingly fit them together. 6. I carved out a space for each stone using a little hand hoe, then I laid them into position. I wore a mask because of the excessive dust. A mighty job, but well worth it—<u>now</u>!

tool's gold

do not feel any workman really likes a new tool. There is always some feeling about it as of something strange and uncongenial, somewhat of the feeling that David had about Saul's armour." (Thank you, Gertrude Jekyll—my sentiments exactly!) Born in London in 1843, Miss Jekyll, as she was known all her life, shared her philosophy on tools in *Home and Garden*, first published in England in 1900. To enjoy her entire gardening credo, search for early editions of *Home and Garden* or any of her thirteen books at a good secondhand bookstore—as she would have preferred!—or check your local library. If you're inclined to start your own collection, most of her books are still in print.

But first, turn back to pages 26–27, and share the Jekyllian kind of joy I experienced a year ago at a huge tag sale, turning a corner and finding—as if a drill sergeant had just barked, "Ten-shun!"—the most heroic lineup of veteran rakes, shovels, hoes, scythes, and ladders. As I passed down the line (muttering a soft "At ease!" as I went), I scrutinized every detail, from the well-worn pegs of an old wooden hay rake, seen at the center of page 27, to the seemingly frivolous blue paint—a gardener's signature—on the rectangular spade of a workhorse shovel, seen on page 26, at the extreme left. I couldn't resist the blue shovel, a digging hoe branded the same color, and an old D-handled spading fork with a more subtle Andrew Wyeth kind of blue rubbed into its old wooden shaft (seen in its new home, page 35), and another lineup of hand tools—pruning shears and clippers—seen on pages 30–31. The total for all came to $10!

I must admit that I am constantly tempted by the shiny new, ergonomically designed garden tools of today (I even own some!), but there's something about grasping the worn handle of some other gardener's well-loved and used old wooden-handled trowel. Miss Jekyll would agree wholeheartedly: "When the knife that has been in one's hand and/or one's pocket for years has its blade so much worn by constant sharpening that it can no longer be used, with what true regret does one put it aside, and how long it is before one can really make friends with the new one!" Broken-in does not, after all, mean broken.

Clockwise from top left: 1. In 1903, Helena Rutherfurd Ely, an American gardening disciple and writer, inventoried the ideal tool room in *The Woman's Hardy Garden*. Gardening gloves, allowing the most freedom of movement, were essential. Those with "clumsy finger-tips" were to be avoided at all costs. The pair, seen here, for kids, was found last Christmas in the barn at Muskettoe Pointe Farm. Their faded color indicates they've lived through quite a few gardening seasons. The distressed paper tag, still attached, suggests they've never been worn! Could clumsy finger-tips be the cause? **2.** Perfect bouquet for a gardener—a hand fork (see it restored on page 31), a trowel, and various wood and metal cultivators—picked out of a jumble at A–Z Swap, Clearwater, Florida, for a grand total of $2.50. **3.** Precursor to the mechanical grass trimmer (I call them weed-whackers)—the sickle. A dozen tied up with raffia and sold as an instant collection for $35, at Northeast Antiques, in Millerton, New York. **4.** Stamped metal tools dating from the 1920s and 1930s, like the red claw displayed with other hand tools in a clay pot at The Garden Room at Provence Art & Antiques, Belleair Bluffs, Florida, are thinner and more likely to rust than their forged counterparts.

I came, I saw, I hoarded the four pairs of clippers flanked by two pairs of secateurs (the English term for pruners) at a tag sale in upstate New York. Average cost: $1.50.

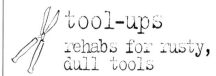

tool-ups
rehabs for rusty, dull tools

I collect rusty old clippers, shears, and pruners, not only because I admire their integral design, but because I truly enjoy putting them back to work. Here's how to do it:

Rust Rehab: Surface rust can be eliminated with steel wool and a lot of elbow grease. My neighbor Bob Albig supervised a deeper cleaning of the rusty garden fork, seen above (before and after the job), with an electric wire brush attached to his bench grinder. For hard-to-reach inside edges he used a hand speed drill with a wire brush attachment. Use extreme caution when cleaning or sharpening edged tools with an electric grinder. Flying forks or clippers are hazardous to your health!

Stay Sharp: A standard metal file or whetstone can hone most dull edges. Smith & Hawken offers a neat little pair of Eze-Lap Diamond Hone & Stone sharpeners for $12.75.

Squeaky Clean: A little WD-40 squirted between the blades loosens rusted parts, unsticks stuck mechanisms, stops squeaks, and protects the metal.

Maintenance: The trick is to keep those reborn tools fit. To prevent any earthy moisture from turning to rust, fill a bucket with sharp builder's sand, moistened with motor oil, and, after a tool is used, knock off loose dirt and plunge it in. Wipe off any excess oil and store tools in a dry place.

Ellen O'Neill's home is in New York City, but her heart is in the little house and piece of ground she recently purchased in a seaside village just off the beaten track from the bright lights and din of the Hamptons. If you read *American Junk* (now a Penguin Studio paperback for $19.95), you should greet her like an old friend. She shared many treasures with us then, and one was the basket seen at left. It was last featured (see *American Junk*, page 99) in the middle of her kitchen table showcasing old table linens, dish towels, place mats, and napkins—all in shades of pink! She confessed then that its Achilles heel was a rather big hole in the bottom that had never posed a problem, "because we never moved it . . . it was a permanent fixture." After its move to the new house, it was moved once more, to Ellen's little mudroom (see pages 52–53), where it catches odds and ends from her gardening life—all green this time!

Left: A closer look reveals, clockwise, from lower left: **1.** A rusty green claw that reminds Ellen of "a bony hand," $3, from a cache of tools lugged back from Pennsylvania. **2.** A ball of twine—"for tying up vines," and a green vintage volume—*America's Garden Book*, $2 from Sage Street Antiques, Sag Harbor, New York. **3.** A supine stack of clay pots from "all over for almost nothing" and a pair of blue clippers, also $3, also from that Pennsylvania cache —extremely vital to her because she'll never own a weed-whacker—"They scare me, they smell, and they make much too much noise."

Above: My sister Liza at work with a long-handled spading shovel. Its angled head makes it the perfect tool for picking up soil, moving it from place to place, and—when a foot is applied in the right place—it's a great digger.

Excess should be condoned when it comes to collecting a genre like tools. Recently I was astounded by a photograph of a whitewashed wall of rusty tools, mostly fragments, collected by a young man in South Africa. He took as much care with his exhibition as a museum curator presenting the rare artifact of a historic dig. The lesson of these two pages is just the opposite of this, the edification of one. One humble shovel, at work above, becomes at rest, at right, a sculptural object, an icon to good and useful work.

Far right: The D-handled (so named because it's shaped like the letter D), four-tined spading fork is required equipment for gardeners worth their soil! My motivation was based on less utilitarian requirements—I loved the faded blue color of the shaft. Leaning solitarily against the weathered wooden door of the Garden Hutte, it reminds me of an Andrew Wyeth watercolor.
Right: At rest, a D-handled vintage version of the spading shovel my sister Liza puts to work at top.

Right: The rake rack outside the shuttered entrance to the Garden Hutte is a handy catchall for, from left to right: a vintage hand fork with red twisted tines, $3, Amenia Auction Gallery, Amenia, New York; a miniature broom, $1, Tomorrow's Treasures, Pleasant Valley, New York; a child's faded blue-and-white cloth parasol, $2, Copake Country Auction, Copake, New York; a wire plant frame and assorted bamboo support stakes.

rake rack

It was my friend Gloria Landers, on a junking expedition through the Smoky Mountains region of North Carolina, who slipped me the tip on rake racks. We spent the good part of a day weeding through tons of old tools until she found two steel rake heads that met her special requirements—not too rusty, not too bent, and not too pricey. They were a quarter each!

When we returned to her cozy retreat up a mountainside, she proceeded, after giving each a good rub (with steel wool) and scrub (with a wool soap pad in hot water), to hang the first on her kitchen wall, and wedge between the teeth a collection of her favorite kitchen utensils.

The other one was attached to the wall outside her husband Sam's garden shed—inspiration for the one outside my Garden Hutte (at right), made out of the already handle-less straight rake shown at top on the opposite page. I secured it to my Garden Hutte wall (metal stem down) using three heavy-duty brads (nails are fine, too) hammered in at either end and one in the middle. Take advantage of the curvilinear shape of a bow rake—like the one at far right, still attached to its blue handle—and hang the head bow side up.

Above: Rakes and rake heads are easy prey at flea markets and yard sales. The bow rake, on the right, designated by the shape of the metal bowing from the teeth to the shaft, is used to rake soil in the garden. It was $3 at a local yard sale. The rake head, to its left, $1, from the Elephant's Trunk Flea Market, New Milford, Connecticut, from a straight rake, is used for lawn leveling.

Number one reason for buying a broken rake? The do-it-yourself rake rack, seen on the opposite page. Rakes have combed the surface of the earth since the days of ancient China, Greece, and Rome. It wasn't until the sixteenth century that they got all their teeth. And, it wasn't until the Victorian Age, when lawns became king, that their varieties flourished. The flexible wire rake was advertised as a lawn broom. It was lightweight and a dream to use. (Still is!) The rakes seen above are steel-tined, no-nonsense garden rakes—the real taskmasters of the garden.

Left: My friend Teddi, a fellow gardener from Virginia, has a rake just her size. The best way to discourage a young gardener is to insult her with plastic toy tools or frustrate her with cumbersome adult-sized tools. A spade, a fork, and a rake are a good starter set. Check garden catalogues or shops for options. Smith & Hawken offers a three-piece, scaled-down version of their regular Bulldog line for $75.

The glory of the galvanized watering can began with the Victorian gardener. Though the upper class had their conservatories and a multitude of fancy watering vessels to serve their pampered buds, the masses wanted something sturdy to help them get the job done in the outdoors. The one they chose, and most gardeners still consider the classic, was made of steel sheet metal protected from rust by a dipping in molten zinc. The detachable sprinkling head was dubbed a rose. Rose was not what I was thinking when I saw the mashed-up head of the watering can seen above. It looked like some sort of exotic mushroom to me. Many old cans, like the two to the right of it, have been deflowered (lost their roses!), which makes them not only less collectible, but certainly less serviceable. If an old watering can is in your future, make sure to check for leaks.

Clockwise from above: 1. Driving down a country road in upstate New York I spied (and coveted!) a painted plywood "Little Miss Mary" watering a giant sunflower (only the leaves are visible, in the upper right corner) with the garden classic—a galvanized watering can. **2.** The kind of sign that makes a junker's heart beat faster—"50% off." I picked up the galvanized siphon for 25 cents, to display with my galvanized watering cans, seen below. **3.** A galvanized militia of zinc-cured watering cans, plus the siphon I bought for a quarter (seen above) is stored on a shelf in our barn. Current status: retired from active duty!

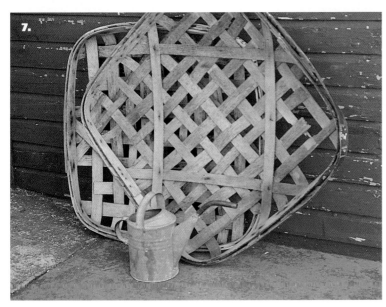

Clockwise from top left: 4. It was the dead of winter when I picked out this watering can from the wonderful garden clutter of Tag Tale Antiques, exhibiting in New York City at The Garage during the winter, and in Southampton, New York, when things warmed up. Why did I buy? For the faded green paint and the circled star branded on the spout, and the price—$10. **5.** Bob Albig, our neighbor in the country, has many talents. Another one was recently revealed when I questioned him about this long-necked copper watering can resting on a stone wall in his yard: "Oh, I made that about 35 years ago," he humbly asserted. Add tinsmith to his list. **6.** Another Albig watering can, specially crafted out of galvanized sheet metal over forty years ago. The big beaklike spout was originally designed to pour water into big truck radiators. **7.** Another deflowered watering can stands alone in front of a backdrop of two oversized shallow wooden slatted trays. They resemble what we call, in Virginia, tobacco baskets. The can was $3, the baskets $12 each, at The Hen Nest, Seminole, Florida.

Every weekday morning at around seven, I leash up Bo, our wirehaired fox terrier, ride the elevator down twelve floors, and head out across Madison Avenue toward Park. I have taken this walk for nine years and know the rows of houses like the back of Bo's paw. There are elegant old brownstones with carved stone urns stationed at their pristine entrances. Window boxes painted the perfect green are filled with tall red geraniums and spill over frothy vines of ivy. High-rises anchor the corners of each block. They tower over the brownstones like mighty centurions. I admit a small prejudice against these big buildings. For me, they have always been icons of an impersonal city life. However, my vision is changing. One day I noticed a burst of green in a fourth-floor window. It was a veritable jungle of succulents flourishing on an interior windowsill. Next to it, below it, and above it were more interior gardens—hanging pots, trees, even window-sized trellises. Now when I pass a high-rise I look again and see instead a towering greenhouse.

Far left, top: Necessary to sustain gardens on the inside—a red plastic watering can that has survived dog teethings and other hazards of indoor gardening life. I bought it <u>new</u> at one of those "dollar" stores.

Far left, bottom: After a small paint job, save the can and make your own pint-sized watering can. Someone else created this one. Very appreciative, I bought it for $5, at the Amenia Auction Gallery, Amenia, New York.

Left: Indoor gardeners depend on smaller watering cans with longer spouts for splashless hits. Two for the job: a rose-embossed metal version and a yellow sidekick, both found at Penny Paid, Locust Hill, Virginia, for $1 and 50 cents, respectively.

Above: A dangerous sign for junkers at the wheel. My bumper sticker spells out a cautionary "I Brake for Junk." See it on page 5.

The bouquet of coreopsis stuck in the galvanized pitcher on the opposite page is a pretty fair demonstration of my flower-arranging prowess. Though I have a certain fringe awareness of those underwater secret weapons that serious floral designers employ, I have never (other than a brief brush with a block of green oasis, florist's foam), quite frankly, bothered. What we're talking about is flower frogs (so named because they sit in the water!)—underwater security systems for stems. They date back to fourteenth-century Japan, and come in endless varieties. Two workhorse versions are seen at the right and on the opposite page. If flower arranging is not a priority, collect these stem holders, as I do, to stem the tide of papers (as a paperweight!) and pencils (as a pencil holder!) on my Garden Hutte desk.

Right: My "free" chair exhibits a miniature cache of garden artifacts scooped up from a flea market table for less than $10.
Opposite: A phalanx of flower frogs—two glass, one galvanized—overseen by a green garden elf, a gift from a veteran gardener.

pot luck

I'm almost certain it was my brother Jimmie, at age eight, who discovered the mushy clay deposits at the foot of the sandy banks down by the Rappahannock River in front of Muskettoe Pointe Farm, our home in Virginia. Thus began one of the messiest traditions of our childhood. Careening down the hills out of control, he probably leapt right into the clay feet first. It was gray and cold and slimy. It squished up between our toes and through our fingers. We (there are nine of us—seven girls, two boys!) mined great blobs of it with our hands. My sister Liza molded little gray pots set out in lumpy little rows. At the end of the day they were baked (like us) by the sun, and though they didn't resemble the color or the shape of many of the clay pots to come in this chapter, their origins were not that different.

If I had come upon them the day I filled the bushel basket, at left, with pot luck stuff from Tomorrow's Treasures in Pleasant Valley, New York, you would see them nestled in with what I did find, detailed in the caption below. Collecting the terra-cotta clay pot, the gardener's classic, is easily accomplished by scouring junkyards and yard sales just about anywhere; the real fun (and challenge) is hunting down oddball containers like the finger-painted art school castoff seen in the basket at left, or a child's vintage tin sand pail, or a collection of pastel stovepipe hat-shaped sap buckets like those seen on pages 54–55, or my favorite of all make-do-with-what-you've-got pots—an aluminum tea kettle and water pitcher serving up thriving crops of *Echeveria glauca*. (Check it out on page 58.) Pots are so democratic. . . and poetic. Reshaping their destiny by filling them with soil and seeds is incredibly satisfying and unquestionably thrifty. If you don't have a plot, you can plant it in a pot.

Left: A potluck stew of tomorrow's treasures from a store by the same name in Pleasant Valley, New York. The pot picked to stir up such savory items as a quartet of 4½-inch blue, pink, white, and black clay pots sprouting a pair of green metal cypress trees hijacked from a toy train set, a two-handled pot painted in swirly pastels, and a green lily pad (or is it a cucumber?) plate beneath the heap. A ubiquitous oval box (see it again on page 95, and <u>again</u> in the garden tent on page 79), blooming hand-painted roses and tulips on its lid, is, in fact, an old produce basket painted red, white, and green. (See it in its afterlife on page 72, at the doorway to my heavenly garden tent.) All of this and so much more (see the so much more on page 98, Floral Fakes) totaled in at $150. This tasty serving was a bargain for $10, <u>not more</u>!

Clockwise from right: 1a. Two varieties of tropical plants bloom in front of the pink Banyan Tree in Clearwater, Florida—to the right of the blue steps are two large pots of *Codiaeum*, and to the left (seen close up, **1b** below) a single potted plant that will never need watering, created out of painted metal. A plant I can't kill (hurray!) for $15. **2.** Do-it-yourself painted clay pots in blue, pink, and red set in a swirly wire plant stand painted yellow create a strange torso for the papier-mâché cat's head propped on top (see later on my scaredy cat scarecrow, page 113). Just part of a winning cache of stuff found at Tomorrow's Treasures, Pleasant Valley, New York, described in detail on page 47. **3.** Memory jars, studded with the personal memorabilia of their makers, I am familiar with; but never before had I come across what I'd call memory pots. Some zealous artisan/gardener encrusted these two clay pots with everything from costume jewelry to an old shell collection, with a few cannibalized doll heads stuck on for measure. I plopped down $30, without blinking, at the Elephant's Trunk Flea Market, New Milford, Connecticut. **4.** Stumbled upon at A–Z Swap, Clearwater, Florida, three viable candidates, at 25 cents each, for plants in the home. Turn to page 56 for how to drill drainage holes. **5.** Gardening ingenuity displayed on an old stoneware crock handpainted with wraparound tulips. It was discovered in the cavernous back room of Lord Botetourt Antiques, Gloucester Court House, Virginia, for $8. (Don't let the formal name or front rooms intimidate you!) **6.** From the Garden Room at Provence, Belleair Bluffs, Florida, a green and brown glazed jardiniere embossed with spiky details. (Looks like majolica, to me.)

1a.

1b.

2.

5.

3.

4.

6.

Clockwise from left: 7. A pair of old wire baskets, $2 each, aided my shopping for clay pots at Stan'z Used Items & Antiques, Kingston, New York. Later the baskets became the perfect portable storage solution for the pots on the floor of the Garden Hutte; see page 20. **8.** A pair of potted not-so-very succulents transplanted to a different kind of jungle environment at J's Odds & Ends, Largo, Florida, thrive on a mountain of old lawn chairs, rubber hoses, and the scrap metal equivalent of garden weeds. **9.** Fertile grounds for finding everything from clay pots (seen at top on the window ledge), to second-hand mowers, seen on page 165, to a floral masterpiece, seen on page 104—J's Odds & Ends, Largo, Florida. **10.** A mosaic pot pieced together like a patchwork quilt out of tiny crockery fragments, $3 at a Lime Rock, Connecticut, flea market. **11.** A cast-iron cooking collection abandoned by a fed-up cook was purchased by a hopeful gardener for $30 at Tomorrow's Treasures, Pleasant Valley, New York. (She saw six pots for plants—not *pot-au-feu!*) How to drill holes in cast iron is her biggest worry! **12.** A tower of three clay pots mottled by pastel paints left too long in the outdoors appears to be part of an Impressionist-like flower painting framed behind them. See it and them in their Garden Hutte home on page 20. **13.** Lora Zarubin has a double passion for old pots and picture frames. In her New York City apartment they are "on vacation," and function purely as works of art. The unusual ridged terra-cotta pot used to collect maple syrup from trees was found at Mädderlake, New York City, for $20. The frame from a Paris flea market was $10.

Above: A pair of park benches, $35 each, at Stan'z in Kingston, New York.
Right: An eight-pointed woodcut star, $10, a Copake, New York, tag sale treasure, also seen on page 25.

Last June, the eleventh to be exact, I had had enough. The Garden Hutte was well under way, the new door had been cut, eight new windows fit, a stone floor had been laid, upon which chairs and a bench were strategically placed to appreciate a view of gardens and a new picket fence. <u>What</u> gardens? Well, exactly. (Turn back to page 25 and share my frustration!) There had been no time to plan or plant a garden. So, it was <u>that</u> day I got into my truck and headed to Copake to my favorite little nursery. I coursed through beds and greenhouses dodging hanging pots like a ravenous twister. When the dust settled, the truck was filled with flats of herbs and pots of old-fashioned annuals. Two of my favorites, purple coneflowers and hollyhocks, were replanted immediately into roomy clay pots, seen at right.

It was a moment in my junking history that I won't forget. Late for an auction in Copake (Mike Fallon's Copake Country Auction), I walked through the back door and saw the most beautiful blue primitive cupboard up on the block. Instinctively my hand went up (a dangerous move when you have no idea where the bid is) and then I heard, "Sold to number 42 [my number!] for $125!" (I got lucky that night.) The cupboard, Mike told me later, was found in an old farmhouse in Quebec—also the former home of the gate seen on page 190. Now it's home to nest in my Garden Hutte shed, just a few feet away from the red bench, opposite, where it exhibits a garden variety of receptacles for plants and flowers, interspersed with less functional floral arts.

Left: David Letterman has his "Top Ten" lists; here's my "Top Ten," chosen from the blue cupboard: #1, the zinnia painting on top, $1 from the Methodist Church tag sale in Millerton, New York; #2, the paper parasol in front of it, $3 from the Elephant's Trunk Flea Market, New Milford, Connecticut; #3, on the shelf below, a little wooden bird perched on a well, 75 cents from Collector's Corner, Millerton, New York; #4, the blue glazed "urn" vase, $1, from K & W Antiques, Kilmarnock, Virginia, #5, the green glazed "barrel" vase, to the right of it, $3 from Bottle Shop Antiques, Washington Hollow, New York; on the wall to the right of the cupboard, #6, the portrait of a lady; #7, the pressed butterflies below her; and #8, the watercolor of leafy greens on the bottom shelf of the cupboard at the far left—all from Saint Mary's tag sale held each August in Lakeville, New York; #9, the galvanized hose spinner, $18 from Northeast Antiques, Millerton, New York; and #10, the quartet of wooden shoes lined up on the floor—the green pair with tulips, $20, the mismatched pair, $2—also from Northeast Antiques.

Ellen O'Neill's mudroom (its tale began on page 33) is more like a mud "landing," just up the stairs from the back door of her enchanted cottage in Sag Harbor, New York. Because she makes every inch work for her, she has lined the shelves (cleverly hung over the stairs) with a chorus line of veteran clay pots (some retired from active duty, as you can see!) waiting to be reassigned to some task in the garden, a glimpse of which can be seen through the windows behind them. "Cut Flowers," the green stenciled sign above the screen door, was a surprise find at the Mulford Farm Antiques Show held every summer in East Hampton, New York. ("The show's a little bumped-up for me," says Ellen.) Nonetheless, she came home with a garden souvenir for just $12.

Left: Ellen O'Neill's rusty white mower seen through the screen door; "for smaller jobs" is as she describes it—"like pushing an automobile around the lawn." The lineup of clay pots was courtesy of the plants they formerly held. The little green slatted bench, to the far right of the pots, is to elevate a pot or a person, from Sage Street Antiques, Sag Harbor, New York, for $4.
Below: The flowered hat, circa 1940, was a gift from her aunts—"Summer Sunday Mass Hats," now low-maintenance flowers for Ellen.

Above: A collection of metal sap buckets from Ruby Beets, Bridgehampton, New York, bought for about $25 each as props for an advertising shoot at Elm Glen Farm. They were left behind by a thankful art director, knowing they would be put back to _real_ work (of some kind) on a not-so-real working farm. First chore: collecting autumnal yellow grape vines. To adapt the buckets for plants, drill or carefully punch holes in the bottom for drainage (see page 56 for how-tos).

Here's a perfect example of how you never know. Did I know, when I found the terrifically handy blue metal, rubber-wheeled garden cart, at left, that it would be a match made in heaven with the collection of blue, green, yellow, and lime sap buckets purchased the year before? No, of course not. The cart was purchased at the Lime Rock, Connecticut, Labor Day flea market last Labor Day weekend for $20. When eventually they both ended up in the garden junk chapel of love—my Garden Hutte shed— was I surprised and thrilled? Absolutely! And did I immediately play matchmaker and place the sap buckets into the garden cart? Yes, of course, I did—it was love at first sight. You see, you never know.

I've never met Rebecca Cole, but anyone that can grow what she does out of the oddest beat-up and bedraggled assortment of oil cans, old shoes, porcelain sinks, buckets, and crates is to be liked instantly and without reservation. I first read about her gardening chutzpah in Anne Raver's *New York Times* gardening column. I went immediately to Potted Gardens, Rebecca's flower and antique sanctuary, at 27 Bedford Street, New York City. She was out, according to the nice young man tending the place, tracking down anything green and growing to liven up the place. (It was January!)

Rebecca teaches us no fear: A plant can grow in just about anything as long as it has the right growing medium, correct drainage, and, of course, lots of TLC. Some likely/unlikely candidates are the pair of enamel coffee pots, seen on the corner shelf at right, $3 each at The Second Hand Shop, Geneva, New York, the galvanized watering cans below them, and the little turquoise glazed crock, $3 from Bottle Shop Antiques, Washington Hollow, New York, on the stool to their left.

All can be adapted for growing by drilling or punching drainage holes in their bottoms. Go slowly with an electric drill or use a masonry drill at the slow speed for concrete (like those hanging pots at right), earthenware, or glazed containers. A piece of masking tape over the spot to be drilled will help prevent splintering, and a thick layer of gravel will guard against soggy roots.

Above left: You don't have to go south of the border to find a good, cheap Mexican pot. This one, for $3, and the plastic beaded plant holder it swings from (almost like garden costume jewelry!), for $1.50, were paired up at 22 Junk-A-Tique in Millerton, New York. Just keep in mind that plants in pots have to be watered a lot more often than plants in the ground, because 50 percent of the water evaporates directly through the walls. The good news here is that the blue glaze is not only festive but functional, acting as a moisture barrier over the porous terra-cotta beneath. Bottom line: You don't have to water as often, but don't get lazy.

Above right: My vision of the Hanging Gardens of Babylon does not include plastic hanging pots. This one spotted in a tree at Klutter Korner, Dunedin, Florida, was marked NFS (not for sale), which indicates the proprietors probably had a vision of their own. For certain they had the good sense to know that plastic pots cut down on watering time. If there's a plastic pot in your garden's future, make sure there's a proper drainage hole. Plastic is a snap to drill through using the slow speed of an electric drill. If you go for a porous or nonglazed pot, soak it in clean water overnight to dissolve any harmful salts and to ensure total rehydration. Dried-up old pots are beautiful, but rob the moisture from the soil.

Top: Two lessons in the anything-goes school of plant containment—an aluminum tea kettle and water pitcher perched on a shelf on the side of The Hen Nest (an old hen house converted into an antiques and gifts shop in Seminole, Florida) spouting hearty succulents (*Echeveria glauca*, I think). Succulents, like pinwheels, silver dollar plants, and Christmas cactuses, are perfect tenants for almost any kind of real or alternative plant containers. They seem to thrive on neglect! The wreath hanging above, probably grapevine, entwined and spray-painted white, if given the chance, could offer trellis-like support to the succulent vines dangling below.

Bottom: If a bucket is left outside during a cold spell with even an inch of water in it, the resulting ice will expand, rounding out the bottom, and the pail will never sit flat on the ground again. I know because I've ruined a few good pails and one of my favorite old galvanized tin pitchers this way. Whoever owned the red FIRE bucket, seen at right, before I did shared in the same stupid misfortune. Which is why it and two others, all suffering from different degrees of the same problem, were a bargain at $2. A bucket that rolls on its side when filled with water is not going to do its job, unless, of course, you plant an herb garden in it. I took the less deformed of the three, punched five holes in the bottom, and lined it with about two inches of gravel. (To sog-proof roots, a ratio of two inches of gravel at the bottom for every two feet of pot is a safe bet.) Though I usually just dig up soil from my existing beds, a standard recipe for container gardens calls for one part builder's sand, one part peat moss, one part compost, and two parts loam. My slightly wobbly bucket cradles thyme, sage, and other herbs. When the wind blows the cradle does rock, but so far the baby herbs are content and growing.

Above: According to the 1957 edition of the Montgomery Ward *Farm Book*—"Your Money-Saving Guide To Top Quality Equipment For More Profitable Farming, Better Country Living" (whew!)—the makeshift pot on my makeshift table is a Metal Handle Steel Bushel Basket. Made of heavy-gauge steel, hot dipped, galvanized, rustproof, and leakproof with a seamless drawn bottom, it weighed in at 6 pounds, 8 ounces for $2.89. Thirty-eight years later, mine cost $5, at Bottle Shop Antiques, Washington Hollow, New York. Though Ward recommends it as an ideal feed and silage carrier, I plan to grow sunflowers in mine. The old barn door laid across the two sawhorses, set up outside the Garden Hutte, serves as a sturdy worktable. The stool, just the right height, was $5, also from Bottle Shop Antiques. Unless I get around to reattaching its handle, the fork tines will remain a sculpturesque piece of garden art.

pot holders

Left: This curlicued, two-tiered metal plant stand (also shown on the previous pages) has endured forty coats of paint and almost that many years burdened with plants.
Far left: Outside my Garden Hutte it supports hefty pots of purple coneflowers and hollyhocks. To its right, juggling nasturtiums, is a tall, skinny, albeit rusty, cousin retrieved for $10 from the Elephant's Trunk Flea Market, New Milford, Connecticut.

or those who like to keep their options open, don't have a plot of earth at their disposal, live twenty stories up in a concrete jungle, or simply aren't ready to make a <u>real</u> gardening commitment, plants-in-pots are a happy, but addictive year-round alternative. One pot quickly leads to another, and once the windowsills are full, you need more room on the homefront. No problem. Plant stands, tiered racks, garden carts, and pot hangers are the handy housing alternative. My best home for homeless pots, seen with flowers at left and naked above and on the preceding pages, was, in fact, a gift from neighbors who had stored it in their yard shed for ten years. So, bypass the fancy gardening catalogues and instead dig through garden sheds and basements. Head for yard sales, thrift shops, junk shops, salvage, and wrecking companies. Low-cost plant housing is just around the bend.

Above: A view of our carriage house, the summertime setting for my gardener's garret, seen at far left, and a sleep close to nature.

When spring comes and the weather starts to turn, there is a restlessness that stirs deep in a gardener. We are impatient to live outdoors again. We look forward to long backbreaking days—weeding, planting, mulching, watering. When the last light is gone we are grieved to go inside. Why can't we camp out in our gardens? Pitch our tents among the daylilies? We can, of course, but for those seeking something in-between, consider a gardener's garret. Mine, at left, is set up in our carriage house garage using the space where our truck and garden carts are parked in winter. Everything (except the bedding) was scavenged from flea markets and tag sales. Every detail is meant to provoke sweet dreams for gardeners and non-gardeners alike.

Top: Signs of a gardening life—sun hats, pots of geraniums, and dried delphinium; garden books, a miniature Cotswold cottage, and an everlasting sunflower wreath and grapevines.
Above: A duo of humble, hand-crafted twig plant stands, humbled further by the parched plants they serve outside The Hen Nest in Seminole, Florida. Of the same genus is the wicker stand, seen at far left in the gardener's garret, distinguished not only by its robin's egg blue paint, but by a blooming trophy geranium. From a New England tag sale for $6.

Above and right: Amid the piles of metal detritus at Stan'z Used Items & Antiques in Kingston, New York, I almost missed what has become one of my most precious garden pieces—the little rusty pot holder, seen here, and its mate seen on page 11. The delicate curl of its simple vine and perfectly detailed leaves recalled a necklace Alexander Calder made for his artist wife Louisa, and provoked a memory of another pair of sculptors, Claude and François Lalanne. Known in France as simply Les Lalannes, my friend Marie-France Boyer wrote about them in the May 1987 issue of *World of Interiors*. I dug up the magazine and found not rusty leaves, but Claude's bronzed hostas, garden seats inspired by iris leaves, a clematis brooch, and wisteria necklace. My rusty works of art cost $5, and even *sans* potted flowers, they bloom all year long nailed onto the weathered walls of my Garden Hutte.

Far right: As I gaze at this rusty leaf-scrolled plant stand (just as I found it at a yard sale in upstate New York for $3), I have visions of delicate sculptures. Should I bronze it or weatherproof it with layers of durable Rustoleum? The three-seater below offers a free ride for errant pots.

Clockwise from above: 1. There is no new-owner anxiety about watering plants on a $10 metal outdoor table (1960s?)—an excellent way station for soon-to-be transplanted plants. Here, pots of salvia, white and blue delphiniums, and a pot of stalky purple somethings that remind me of giant chives. **2.** My favorite plant stand (see a close-up on pages 60–61) ablaze with a late summer crop of zinnias, mellowed by pots of herbs. **3.** In the market for something Victorian? Two cast-iron beauties taking some sun in front of the Amenia Auction Gallery in Amenia, New York, both in the $25 range. **4.** From The Garden Room at Provence Art & Antiques, Belleair Bluffs, Florida, "a little old rusty plant stand," as Judy Shoup, owner/seller, puts it. When we went back to negotiate a price, we were told, "Sold!" It went for $34.

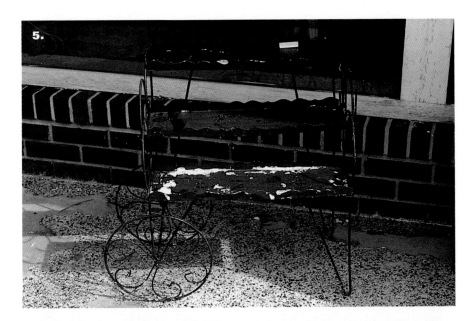

Clockwise from top left: 5. A mobile home of sorts—a garden cart trimmed with cutout leaves, spotted on the street in front of U-Name-It in Watkins Glen, New York. Listed at $5. **6.** Blooming from iron gridwork decorating a 1950s Florida bungalow (now Provence Art & Antiques) is a perfect pot of vines—no watering required. Sometimes these houses get dismantled and you can find their leftovers at local salvage and wrecking companies. From ornate garden trim to gates, shutters, and such, it's a junker's Disneyworld! **7.** Another garden cart. (Wait a minute! Is this the one we saw in Watkins Glen, above, but painted white?) The same, but different. Found at a yard sale in Millerton, New York, for $8.

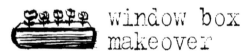

window box makeover

I love wooden flower boxes, except that 1. they're hard to find, and 2. they tend to rot. My solution: go with the plastic boxes, as seen at top (they're hardy, plentiful, and cheap), and camouflage them (the front, at least) with pieces of old wood. The chewed-up green piece, seen above, came from an old wooden flower box that gave up the ghost after years of service. It's secured to the face of the plastic box, shown at top, by a few skinny nails tacked right through.

Clockwise from top: 1. When Kitty Paris bought her dream house, this custom-made wooden flower box, abloom with dahlias, was a gift with purchase. **2.** Judy Shoup, the green-thumb collector behind The Garden Room at Provence, in Belleair Bluffs, Florida, bought this three-tiered wooden stand from an antiques dealer whose husband made it for her in the sixties (a thrifty alternative to a still-hot collectible). **3.** What appears to be a crude toolbox with legs, was a freshly whitewashed gift from René Gomez. It now harbors pots of herbs.

My friend Gloria Landers and I both pounced (the danger of junking with a friend!) on this charming white picketed flower box decorated with a single tulip cutout. It hails from the North Georgia/South Carolina region, according to Judy Shoup, who turned it over to Gloria (I let it go!). I can't reveal the price because it was a birthday present for her husband, Sam (which is why I let it go). Judy suspects it's a composite piece made of an old fence and flower box. She had it hanging on the wall of her Garden Room shop. Instead of planting things in it, Sam could use it as a place to store seed packets and small garden tools. I love the idea of propping several floral paintings in it or one big one—preferably tulips!

Clockwise from top left: 5. A mobile home of sorts—a garden cart trimmed with cutout leaves, spotted on the street in front of U-Name-It in Watkins Glen, New York. Listed at $5. **6.** Blooming from iron gridwork decorating a 1950s Florida bungalow (now Provence Art & Antiques) is a perfect pot of vines—no watering required. Sometimes these houses get dismantled and you can find their leftovers at local salvage and wrecking companies. From ornate garden trim to gates, shutters, and such, it's a junker's Disneyworld! **7.** Another garden cart. (Wait a minute! Is this the one we saw in Watkins Glen, above, but painted white?) The same, but different. Found at a yard sale in Millerton, New York, for $8.

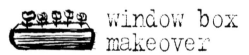

window box makeover

I love wooden flower boxes, except that 1. they're hard to find, and 2. they tend to rot. My solution: go with the plastic boxes, as seen at top (they're hardy, plentiful, and cheap), and camouflage them (the front, at least) with pieces of old wood. The chewed-up green piece, seen above, came from an old wooden flower box that gave up the ghost after years of service. It's secured to the face of the plastic box, shown at top, by a few skinny nails tacked right through.

Clockwise from top: 1. When Kitty Paris bought her dream house, this custom-made wooden flower box, abloom with dahlias, was a gift with purchase. **2.** Judy Shoup, the green-thumb collector behind The Garden Room at Provence, in Belleair Bluffs, Florida, bought this three-tiered wooden stand from an antiques dealer whose husband made it for her in the sixties (a thrifty alternative to a still-hot collectible). **3.** What appears to be a crude toolbox with legs, was a freshly whitewashed gift from René Gomez. It now harbors pots of herbs.

garden camp

hen I dreamed of a garden tent nestled into a favorite green hollow in the woods near our farm in upstate New York, I was dreaming of all the forest hideaways of my childhood, and the book that inspired them—Gene Stratton Porter's *Freckles*. The Limberlost was the mythical Eden-like forest where Freckles, the one-handed orphan who became its guardian, fell in love with a beautiful young girl he called his Angel. My garden tent filled with a naturalist's totems, seen at right and on the preceding pages, is the floral palace he might have created for her. When I go there at the end of a hot summer's day, surrounded by tall grass, low green branches, chittering birds, and a special view of hills and sky, I mouth a silent "Amen" to the peace that only a place like this can bring.

Preceding pages: A movable feast of flora and fauna, my garden tent is a 5½-foot by 6-foot aluminum pole frame tented with a heavy, 100 percent washed cotton fabric (Summer Porch Floral) by Ralph Lauren Home Collection. Specifics on how to create your own Garden Tent follow on page 76.
Right: Under a window cut out and screened with a fabric called "No See-Um Netting" (available at most good fabric stores, or write to Outdoor Wilderness Fabrics Inc., 16195 Latah Drive, Nampa, Idaho 83651) sits a jerry-rigged worktable created out of a skinny 5-foot by 2-foot green door from United House Wrecking in Stamford, Connecticut, for $5, propped on a pair of metal TV trays from Retro in New Milford, Connecticut, for $15. A guided tour of this tabletop garden exhibition begins on page 78.

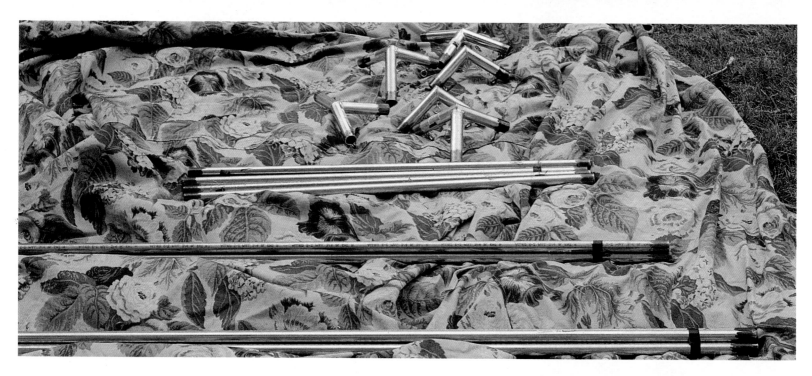

 # tent-nacity—how to get it!

When I decided I had to have a garden tent, I called my friend Gret Warren, a wizard at projects like this, and she gave me the lowdown on how to proceed. My 6-foot-tall stand-up tent frame was constructed out of the EMT pipes seen above (available at most hardware stores in different lengths) connected by corner and peak brackets (found at most good surplus stores). If a custom tent is not what you're up to, consider revamping the frame of an existing camping tent or a beach or garden canopy frame. (Fall is a good time for picking one up at a garage sale.)

There are optional ways to tent your frame. I tented mine with a summer floral of heavy linen—a dream come true when the sun shines on or through it, but a nightmare when it rains. Though Scotchgard and Seam Sealer (a spray campers use to keep water out of their tents and packs) help fortify non-waterproof fabrics, I prefer a rain fly—a waterproof canopy campers stake over their tents. Avoid all this by choosing a waterproof nylon or canvas. Be inventive and paint your own floral fantasy using waterproof acrylics—freehand or with stencils. A quicker way is to seam up some old floral sheets. Your garden tent needn't be incredibly hardy. The idea is a portable palace to retreat to out of the sun within eyeshot of the newest blooms.

Above: All set to go—the fabric of my floral fantasy makes a temporary dropcloth for the pipes and brackets that will support its new life as a portable garden outpost in a shady haven not far from my permanent Garden Hutte just up the hill.

Right: My older son, Carter, my aide-de-camp in yet another garden sortie, takes a well-earned breather in the welcoming shade of our new poppy-and-rose-covered getaway. The table he leans on is actually an old green cupboard door balanced on two TV trays. Turn the page for a behind-the-flaps tour of this kind of garden camp "camp"—and more, much more!

The bones of my garden tent, made of EMT pipes secured at the corners and peaks by brackets, stand 6 feet in the center.

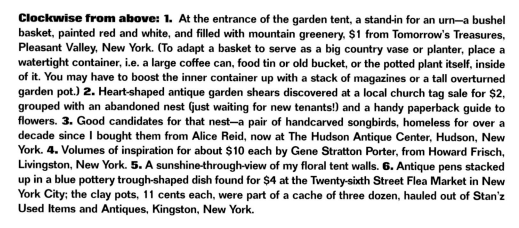

Clockwise from above: 1. At the entrance of the garden tent, a stand-in for an urn—a bushel basket, painted red and white, and filled with mountain greenery, $1 from Tomorrow's Treasures, Pleasant Valley, New York. (To adapt a basket to serve as a big country vase or planter, place a watertight container, i.e. a large coffee can, food tin or old bucket, or the potted plant itself, inside of it. You may have to boost the inner container up with a stack of magazines or a tall overturned garden pot.) **2.** Heart-shaped antique garden shears discovered at a local church tag sale for $2, grouped with an abandoned nest (just waiting for new tenants!) and a handy paperback guide to flowers. **3.** Good candidates for that nest—a pair of handcarved songbirds, homeless for over a decade since I bought them from Alice Reid, now at The Hudson Antique Center, Hudson, New York. **4.** Volumes of inspiration for about $10 each by Gene Stratton Porter, from Howard Frisch, Livingston, New York. **5.** A sunshine-through-view of my floral tent walls. **6.** Antique pens stacked up in a blue pottery trough-shaped dish found for $4 at the Twenty-sixth Street Flea Market in New York City; the clay pots, 11 cents each, were part of a cache of three dozen, hauled out of Stan'z Used Items and Antiques, Kingston, New York.

Clockwise from top left: 7. The reward of digging through six boxes of household goods at a Copake Auction tag sale in Copake, New York—the perfect cup for herbal tea (50 cents—and not a chip!) encircled with a delicate ivy border. **8.** A petite watering can constructed out of a pint-sized paint can, decorated with a decal bouquet of roses, cost me $15 at Amenia Auction Gallery, Amenia, New York. The rusty green tin bread box was marked "As is $5," at Bottle Shop Antiques, Washington Hollow, New York, and now stores gardening gloves; the pink poppy metal candlestick holder, to its left, was plucked from a Paris flea market. **9.** A triptych of postcards—Carl Larsson at the top, Monet in the middle, and a feathery flight by a young English artist—serves as lightweight garden pinups. **10.** Remains of my stay—a well-worn, sun-faded chambray work shirt, a crucial part of my gardener's uniform. **11.** A lavender bookmark for required garden reading—Gene Stratton Porter's *Girl of the Limberlost*. **12.** The lacey green garden hat (once a bridesmaid's nightmare?), 50 cents at a local tag sale, camouflages a heavy-duty canvas Outback protector. It was picked up new in a surplus store in Moab, Utah, on the outskirts of the desert.

Taking a daytime nap in the outdoors is a totally seductive idea. So the summer I set up the garden tent I had an urge for a garden cot to make the fantasy real. The cot, one of those official army fold-up kinds, I purchased for $49 from my favorite surplus supplier—Fort Brewster Trading Company in Pawling, New York. I layered it lavishly with soft cotton chambray sheets, pillows, a Swedish army blanket, also from Fort Brewster, $29, and an antique coverlet appliquéed with chenille flowers, bought for $25 years ago from Alice Reid, now in The Hudson Antique Center in Hudson, New York. The experience was seductive, the cot, unfortunately, was not!

art of the vase

Henri Matisse <u>is</u> the indisputable lord of the vase. Take the rusty circle of metal seen on page 171—a discarded table found in a junkyard one cold February a year ago—stroke on swirly layers of green and blue paint, remove it to a sunny garden, place in its center a yellow vase of purple cyclamen, and you come close to re-creating the inspiration for one of his earliest celebrations of this most banal of garden fixtures. *Purple Cyclamen*, painted in 1911, was just the beginning of Matisse's brilliant love affair with this humble container created to enliven and sustain the life of flowers outside the garden. *Still Life with Asphodels*, 1907, is an altar not to one, but to five of these vessels. The central focus of *The Window*, 1916, is a round vase of dainty blue flowers set on a little round table. *Goldfish and Sculpture*, 1912, features a tall green vase of what looks like poppies, a bowl of goldfish, and a reclining nude.

I attribute, not blame, my most outrageous vases to Matisse's bold, spirited use of them. My most prized, at left, displayed reverentially in the Garden Hutte against a landscape propped on its side, was found in a dingy cluttered shed of junk in upstate New York. Its statuesque sixteen inches of heavy clay rise from a base half that size. The scar on its front lip, cutting through the center rosebud, was the result of a fall out of the back of my truck when I first brought it home. (What a welcome!) A little Elmer's glue has healed it almost completely. The basketweave design (out of a mold that shaped many, I'm sure) reminds me of those slightly morbid straw-patterned funeral flower baskets popular in the cemeteries of the Victorian Age. It stands unadorned (except for the painted roses entwined on its top and base), a towering monument to the art of the vase, sustained by its own quirky beauty—with <u>and</u> without flowers!

Left: The rose-embellished basketweave vase, molded of clay and handpainted, was hard to miss, even though the shelf was cluttered and the light dim at Stan'z Used Items & Antiques in Kingston, New York. It cost $20. The field-and-stream landscape tilted vertically behind it, almost like a stage backdrop, gives it the star treatment it deserves. The painting was 75 cents at a church tag sale in Lakeville, New York.

Above: Almost twice as tall as their bizarre sisters, at left, these basketweave vases charmed me at a Copake Country Auction tag sale—$10 for the pair.

Weird pottery is what I'd call these twin sets of vases sprouting three-dimensional, almost grotesque growths of roses (left) and raspberry clusters (above). Are they Baudelaire's *Flowers of Evil* or Eden's forbidden fruit? Some sort of spell must have been cast to charm me into buying these nightmarish vases! Their provenance will never be divulged, nor will my reasons for possessing them. They possess <u>me</u>!

Left: The enchanting pair of rose-covered triple-footed vases, standing about 13½ inches tall, with openings in their throats that would allow only for single stems, were marked $10 a pair at Bottle Shop Antiques, Washington Hollow, New York. Though they appear to be carved out of wood, they are fashioned out of a fragile clay or plaster and texturally painted.

From the turn of the century until the twenties, Goofus Glass—a heavily embossed glass whose trademark colors were reds and greens on bronze and gold grounds—was popularized as carnival prizes. If, however, you didn't win a Goofus Glass set of plates or a creamer and pitcher at your local fireman's carnival, you could buy a Goofus Glass jar filled with pickles at your local general store, finish them off, and have your own prized vase. (For a short time food manufacturers caught on to the trend, bottling some pretty strange products in this funny glass.) Though it's hard to imagine the artful glass vase (right) once storing pickles, I'm almost certain that the two shorter ones did. (Note the extended rim at each mouth designed for a lid to pop on.) What might the taller vase (center) have stored—spaghetti, perhaps? Whatever their former purpose, my prized set, $29 at D's Place, Holland's Stage Coach Markets, Gloucester, Virginia, is now being converted into lamps. I plan to screw in rose-colored bulbs scented heavily with rose oil—just in case the warmth might rekindle those pickle smells of old. The red felt fez, to their right, emblazoned with a gold scimitar (a prize for a Shriner?), was pounced on for $5, at Pat's Attic Treasures, White Stone, Virginia.

The only thing real on these two pages are the rich red roses at left, picked from a climbing vine at Elm Glen Farm, seen on page 198. The faux wooden mug they are arranged in has the look of majolica, but it's not—it's fake! And the bouquet of daisies plunked into the mouth of the (fake!) Lalique glass vase on the opposite page, is, sadly, plastic. Wait, though—in the distance behind the plastic bouquet, slightly out of focus—are those real red and yellow roses? Oh, treachery! They are (say it isn't so) pop-up roses from a novelty card sent from (at last!) a <u>real</u> friend, Marie-France Boyer, sending <u>genuine</u> greetings from Morocco.

Opposite: Lilliputian-sized bouquet of plastic daisies (a gift from my sister Liza) plunked into the mouth of a not-quite-Lalique frosted glass vase (9½ inches tall), embossed with red poppies, $5, from Bottle Shop Antiques, Washington Hollow, New York.
Left: A 6-inch pottery mug mimics the sides of an aged wooden barrel, staves and all. The palm fronds embossed on the front give it the look of majolica, a very collectible glazed earthenware manufactured at the end of the nineteenth century, but the absence of any markings leave its provenance to chance. I bought it anyway about a decade ago for less than $10, from Alice Reid, now selling her wares at The Hudson Antique Center, Hudson, New York.

About ten years ago, I took a train from London to Sussex to visit some dear friends who had retreated to an old farmhouse to paint, sculpt, pot, write, and act. They turned every corner of their new/old home—walls, doors, floors, windows, furniture, fabrics—into an expression of their individual passion for art and life. I took a taxi from the station, but had the driver drop me at the end of the lane to Charleston Farm. I knocked on the first door I came to, and when there was no reply, walked in. "Vanessa? Clive? Duncan? Virginia? Where are you?"

My friends—the artist Vanessa Bell, her good friend and fellow artist Duncan Grant, her husband, Clive Bell, and her sister Virginia Woolf, and the rest of the legendary Bloomsbury group that gathered there—had long since departed. Yet, as I wandered through, I found them all still there in spirit—in a painted chair, a pot, a decorated mantelpiece. My odd collection of pottery and vases, seen here, and on the next few pages was inspired in some intangible way by theirs.

The Omega Workshop Ltd, founded in London in 1913, by Roger Fry with painters Vanessa Bell and Duncan Grant, promoted a kind of English Postimpressionism that lauded the decorative arts in fabrics, furniture, and pottery. The still life, at left, is a little shrine to that last outpost of the Arts and Crafts Movement. The 6-inch, pistachio-colored vase was embossed with a handpainted garden by an Omega artist of our time who has left only a small clue to his or her identity—a minuscule "JJ '88" scratched into the bottom of the vase. From Cindy's Antiques, Amenia, New York, $7.50. The cotton floral bouquet is more recent—from the Ralph Lauren Home Collection.

If I close my eyes and open them on this little pitcher set on a petite tile table, I'm back in the drawing room at Charleston Farmhouse with a pitcher (which I really picked up at the Stormville Airport Antiques Show, Stormville, New York, for $2.50) cast by Quentin Bell (Vanessa's son) and decorated by Duncan Grant. The chipped tile supported by a cast-iron base (from Stan'z, Kingston, New York, $10) was my dream, especially hand-painted for me by Vanessa Bell.

93

Opposite: The best room at Charleston is Duncan Grant's studio. Everywhere you turn there are paintings and pots, hand-painted teacups and tiles, faded floral throw pillows, brilliantly tattered armchairs, decorated lampshades creatively askew, muralized room dividers, jars filled with bunches of marguerites and red-hot pokers, but mostly assorted paintbrushes. It is this poetic clutter that specifically inspired this still-life-in-a-still-life set up in a Charlestonian corner of my Garden Hutte studio. The painting (24 by 17½ inches) of a blue vase of long-stemmed delphiniums and daylilies left me weak in the knees when I found it at the Amenia Auction Gallery, Amenia, New York, for $10. (If Vanessa Bell had painted it, I couldn't have been any happier!) The funny pinched-in-at-the-mouth vase with the blue border of dripping paint equals in my eyes any Omega masterpiece. Though the vase appears to have emerged from the painted still life behind it, it actually emerged off a shelf at Bottle Shop Antiques, Washington Hollow, New York, for $5. The lily pad plate and wooden oval box in the foreground were previewed in a bushel basket of finds on page 46.

Left: One Sunday I took my nephew John Tyler Norton and his sister Mary Randolph Norton to visit the studio of an artist friend of mine, Peter Gee. I don't remember if John Tyler ever took his coat off that day. (It was a cold February day, and artists' lofts can be drafty.) But, as you can see, he certainly had it on when he settled happily into a big comfortable armchair Peter had camouflaged with a large fabric remnant blooming giant blue tulips. Lost in thought, in that jungle of Jurassic Park-sized tulips, John Tyler reminded me of pictures I'd seen of Vanessa Bell's sons, Quentin and Julian, when they were his age. What a portrait she could have made of our John Tyler Norton "Bell"!

floral fakes

have lived with Bonnard at Le Bosquet in a little village high above Cannes, with Matisse at the Hôtel Beau-Rivage looking out at the Promenade des Anglais, with Picasso at Villa Californie and the Château de Vauvenargues, with van Gogh in his little yellow house in Arles. They gave me flowers—mimosas, irises, poppies, sunflowers, wildflowers, roses—bouquets of them, vases of them. I am faithless: I love them all. I tuck tiny postcard reproductions of their gifts in my Garden Hutte, above my desk, in the book I am reading. They're the closest to the real thing I'll ever have. But, never mind, I'm satisfied. I have quenched my thirst with the flowers of the no-name Impressionists of the flea markets. I scour, I dig, I leap at any honest attempt. My garden gallery is full.

Left: These three no-name Impressionist still lifes, plus seven others, six garden hats, a broom, Christmas ornaments, a papier-mâché cat mask, a large produce basket, four vases, seven flower pots, and a tiny log cabin totaled in at $150 at Tomorrow's Treasures, Pleasant Valley, New York.

Preceding pages: A bouquet worthy of Bonnard, picked from my summer garden and prodded into a blue enamel coffee pot plucked from a flea market outside of Paris! At right, a Garden Hutte corner crammed with eclectic garden arts. The rather formal still life of roses wedged along the beam at upper left was found, along with another of daylilies and snowballs (propped in the lower right corner), at Cindy's Antiques in Amenia, New York, for $5 apiece. The cartoon-like painting of orange and yellow daisies, the trellis-like plastic hot-plate pitcher, and a pale green double, dipping above, were all found at the Rummage Shoppe in Millerton, New York. Postcard works of art were collected at the Metropolitan Museum of Art, New York City.

At the top of my top ten list of things to grow is a tall, exotic stalky plant with a large fuzzy spherical flower cluster that looks something like a purple porcupine. This is allium. Being botanically unsophisticated, I could not swear to the genus of the tall skinny blossoms seen in the painting at right and on the preceding pages. Is it allium or just a good old home-grown bouquet of leeks like those seen at the far right, blooming resolutely in my neighbors' garden? Whatever they are, they are now mine, and live year-round in my Garden Hutte, not far from the real thing—leeks or allium—which will both bloom any day now in my dream garden just around the corner.

Right: Allium, leeks, giant chives, globe-thistle, or gone-to-seed dandelions? These mystery blooms swirl dramatically out of a delicate glass vase (seen in entirety on page 98), part of a great flora and fauna cache unearthed at Tomorrow's Treasures in Pleasant Valley, New York. Painted by Mita O. in 1987, it cost me about $5.
Far right: Unquestionably, these are flowering leeks planted the spring before by Elsie and Bob Albig, our green-thumbed neighbors in the country. "I wintered these over," Elsie told me. "They never blossom the first year." The payoff was certainly worth the wait. The stalks were over four feet tall in their prime. Elsie presented them to me at the end of the season. They dry beautifully.

Above: A summer tenant residing in my family's cottage on the Outer Banks of North Carolina penned in our guest book a vaguely derisive comment about our "attic" art. A family veto ruled against guest books from that day on! Possibly the glass bowl of drooping peonies didn't meet with her approval. It was lovingly selected for $2 from one of our favorite hunting haunts—Pontes Antiques in Kill Devil Hills, North Carolina.

Right: The vision at left comes to life on our summer porch in upstate New York. I live in fear of missing the weekend the peonies bloom. Though this pitcher seems to call for tulips, it's a perfect depth and width to hold the heavy blossoms at bay. I uncovered it years ago in a shop run by my friend Alice Reid for $12. Today her treasures are packed into several spaces at The Hudson Antique Center in Hudson, New York.

The gardens I fall in love with seem to be totally unpremeditated, as though their architects were the wind, birds, and some slightly eccentric combination of Gertrude Jekyll, Vita Sackville-West, and Claude Monet. They are totally out of control, and totally passionate, mixing every species of formal flower with herb, wildflower, and weed. Since I am still working on _that_ garden for myself, I gratify my fantasy by landscaping my walls the way I would a garden plot, haphazardly sowing weeds and roses, watercolors and oils, framed and unframed canvases—a Matisse postcard with a 50-cent flea market master. It's all in the mix.

Opposite left: A spring bouquet of richly burnished tulips is stark against the artist's dark canvas. Several tears did not deter me. For $4 at the Copake Country Auction tag sale, Copake, New York. The chair, its painted pedestal, was free! (See it also on page 44.)
Opposite right: J's Odds & Ends in Largo, Florida, is a little piece of junker's heaven. Mostly stacked with large machinery and furniture (see more on pages 49 and 165), this delicate still life painted by Helen Rogers in 1945 (a hybrid daisy called _Gazania_ according to my Burpee's Gardens catalogue) was a big surprise! I had to dicker for $10.
Left: My friend Kevin de Martine, owner of Bottle Shop Antiques in Washington Hollow, New York (a bottle's throw from Millbrook), has a good eye for bottles, but a really _great_ eye for paintings. Some of my most unusual have come from him. In the flower category, these are not atypical, but the top one, painted in 1948 by E. M. Berling has a spatial incongruity and a turquoise table that I love (12 by 16 inches for $16). The daylilies (9 by 12 inches for $17) were painted by Mabel Rittenhouse for her friend Adah Hall. Kevin had the two works exhibited together. His curatorial skills are superb as well!

105

gimme shelter

In my Gardeners' Hall of Fame I would place Gertrude Jekyll, Vita Sackville-West, Beverly Nichols, Carl Larsson, Pierre Bonnard, Henri Matisse, Vincent van Gogh, Georgia O'Keeffe, . . . Elizabeth (author of *Enchanted April* and *Elizabeth's German Garden*), and Maria Hofker. The latter, I met through *Le Jardin enchanté de Maria Hofker*, a very special book filled with watercolors of Hofker's flowers, written by Marie-France Boyer and published in France (Chêne, 1988). In the introduction there is a photograph of Maria, a woman over ninety years of age—a gardener and watercolorist—sitting amid her roses, Japanese anemones, phlox, rows of delphinium, and flowering shrubs. She is shaded by a delicate antique parasol attached to her little white painting table and a large-brimmed straw hat secured at the crown with a black-and-white polka-dotted kerchief. It is a moment that clarifies for me everything that I love about gardening and gardening hats—their allure, romance, fantasy, and art.

Van Gogh painted himself at least a dozen times in a straw hat. He probably found them agreeable not only for their protection (he was a fair redhead) but for their heritage as well. Straw hats were part of the peasant's daily uniform. Vita Sackville-West was painted by William Strang (in 1918) in a vivid green silk jacket, yellow skirt, and wide-brimmed red hat. She was twenty-six. I have searched for a photograph I know I have seen showing her many years later on the steps of Sissinghurst. She had just trudged in from her beloved gardens and was wearing jodhpurs, green Wellies, and a wide-brimmed straw hat. My neighbor Bob Albig is seen on the following page in his latest garden topper—a straw beachcomber's hat, spiffed up with a faded madras band and an imposing turkey feather. He recently retired his favorite farmer's straw hat and donated it to my Garden Hutte collection (a sampling of which is seen at left). In the spring and summer I wave to him as he rides his trusty tractor-mower, dressed in red-suspendered jeans, a workshirt rolled to the elbows, and always the hat—the jewel in the crown of the gardener's costume.

Left: It wasn't garden hats that Mick Jagger was singing about in "Gimme Shelter," popularized in the sixties, but it certainly applies. The straw tower of six stacked up on a wrought-iron chair (seen in full on page 182) was collected from various sales and shops. At the top, looking a bit like an English boater wrapped in a striped tie, a $1 find from Tomorrow's Treasures in Pleasant Valley, New York. The preppy version below tied up with a madras bow and fake daisy was spotted at Martha's Mixture in Richmond, Virginia, one of a funky pair for $5.

Clockwise from above: Bob Albig, my neighbor in the country, stopped by the Garden Hutte last summer to say hello and present me with a well-worked straw "farmer's" hat he had recently retired. It now is part of the permanent collection displayed in the Garden Hutte, and seen close up at top right. Below it, a banana-leaf special festooned with plastic cocktail stirrers (probably a souvenir from a Caribbean vacation) was the first of a quartet of hats collected one Sunday for $20 from the Elephant's Trunk Flea Market in New Milford, Connecticut.

Opposite: A child's Victorian hat, the second of a quartet found at Elephant's Trunk for $20, rests on a scalloped gold-and-white wooden table picked up on that same Sunday in the same field at the Elephant's Trunk Flea Market for just a few dollars. One of the legs fell off before I got it to the car. Until I glue it securely, let's hope nothing heavier than the hat lands there!

Clockwise from above: 1. Drive north through Salisbury, Connecticut, and you'll see Flo (short for Flower), a very lifelike, life-size doll sitting pretty in the back of an old pickup. Her job is to promote a visit to the Salisbury Antique Center, where (if you're lucky) you'll find a hat like hers! **2.** The third of the quartet of hats found for $20 at the Elephant's Trunk Flea Market in New Milford, Connecticut. It hangs on its own chin string—a perfect purple foil among purple coneflowers (*Echinacea*). The little tree-bark birdhouse to its right was from Stan'z Used Items & Antiques, in Kingston, New York, for $20. **3.** It wasn't easy to pass by Arline Dunlop's booth at the Elephant's Trunk Flea Market in New Milford, Connecticut. Her lime green net cap was a real show-stopper, but not for sale— and certainly <u>not</u> for gardening! **4.** An $8 triple threat pot holder from Tomorrow's Treasures, Pleasant Valley, New York, works a double shift as a hat stand for a gardener's pink tophat blooming little clumps of straw flowers for $6 from Retro, New Milford, Connecticut. **5.** A farmer's straw hat, similar to the one Bob Albig gave me (see page 108), decorated with a bouquet of freshly picked salvia, which will dry and last forever. The hat was 50 cents from a nearby tag sale.

Clockwise from top left: 6. Snapped on Easter Sunday at my family's home in Virginia, a little stone pug ($40 at King William Antiques, Toano, Virginia) decked out for the occasion in a buttercup bonnet which later disappeared and mysteriously showed up at church on the head of one of my young (and very enterprising) nieces. **7.** Looking a bit like a decorated officer from the Foreign Legion, a faded blue pith helmet (the fourth of the four for $20 from the Elephant's Trunk Flea Market) on top of a hat stand in the Garden Hutte draped with a junker's vest (see junker's garb, page 4) and an official green sash with Girl Scout badges, $5, at Cindy's Antiques in Amenia, New York. **8.** Almost good enough for the races at Ascot, a classic straw round-brimmed hat braced with a red pompon from Collector's Corner in Millerton, New York—a $2 prize! **9.** A psychedelic gardener (my older son, Carter) decked out in a tie-dyed T-shirt (a personal project) and his father's favorite beach hat. **10.** Welcoming all who enter The Banyan Tree in Largo, Florida, a little Miss Pinky in a very big hurry under a very big schoolgirl's hat (not unlike the ones Madeline and her classmates wore in that wonderful story by Ludwig Bemelmans).

The traditional scarecrow was symbolically delegated authority through the worn-out clothes, and particularly the hat, passed down to it by the farmer. But, if you believe the latest bird-scaring research claiming that birds are less scared of these imitations of the human form than they are of things that rattle, flash, and move, then my garden is doomed, and my scarecrow seen at right (dressed in <u>my</u> shirt, gloves, and a souvenir hat from Curaçao) is a useless monument to the past, lost to high-tech pesticides and a new robocop breed of scarecrows. The winner of the Effaroucheur (scarer) class of the Third Annual Scarecrow Competition (at the Potager du Roi in Versailles last June) was just such a creature cut out of highly reflective metal with bladelike propeller arms. The good news is there was another winner, judged completely on artistic impression! If then I string together a necklace of tin can tops and snap-off soda can tabs, and throw it around the neck of my scarecrow along with a sash of aluminum foil around her hat, have I beat the research, the competition—<u>and</u> the birds?

Right: A scarecrow battles birds and the elements, so wardrobe selection is key. The floppy but practical straw souvenir was $5 from Tomorrow's Treasures in Pleasant Valley, New York.
Opposite: A scarecrow's spare hat hung up in the rafters of the Garden Hutte with a spare bedroom for a bird nearby. Below, a lineup of floral fakes (chapter of them begins on page 96), from left to right—an Italian pottery urn, a still life of anemones, and drooping paper tulips—all found at local flea markets for under $5.

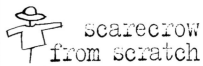

scarecrow from scratch

Here's how I made my scarecrow, more of a "scaredy cat" than robocop, seen below and at far left.

Take a long, sturdy stick (mine was approximately 6 feet) and nail or fasten with rough twine a shorter crossbar behind it. Stake it into the ground and dress with an old shirt or jacket. Stick thinner branches up the sleeves (unless your crossbar fills them) and dress the "fingers" with old garden gloves. Create a head out of a dried gourd and a stuffed cloth bag (you paint the face), or find one ready to go like I did. Secure it on the top of the stick with wire. (My cat head was hollow so I just plopped it on.) The finishing touch is a formidable hat stylishly secured, if need be, with more wire. This is a 15-minute project—the way I like them!

Above: A frontal view of my scarecrow reveals why I dubbed her the "scaredy cat" scarecrow! The papier-mâché head (scary except for the charming pink ears) was a drama school project, found with the hat at Tomorrow's Treasures for $1.

Harshly tattooed with their prices—$10 and $5—these two little dolls found together at Bottle Shop Antiques in Washington Hollow, New York, are breathtakingly fashionable in tattered print dresses, red lips, and the striking straw *chapeaux.* They stand 7 inches and 8 inches tall. The little one on the left is twice the price of her taller sister because she is, in fact, quite a bit older (looks <u>can</u> <u>be</u> deceiving!). She is plaster; her sister is plastic. They remind me of those beautiful girls Henri Lartigue would photograph in the twenties, strolling along the boardwalk in Deauville.

flower power

flower power

ears ago I resigned myself to living with the illusion of a garden rather than having the real thing. First of all, I chose to live in a big city, and though there are many who have found ingenious ways to garden on rooftops, balconies, fire escapes (albeit illegally), in window boxes, and on overcrowded windowsills, I've never been particularly lucky or perhaps dedicated enough to be successful. To this day, other than a doggedly determined ficus tree (only my second in twenty years!), my city flora and fauna bloom from works of art (see page 97), fabrications on furniture, pillows, lampshades, at windows, on plates and pottery and from all sorts of flowery bric-a-brac. Several years ago I spied my answer to drooping flower arrangements—fantastic stalks of pink, yellow, and green water lilies arranged in a graceful pedestal and all carved of wood (see number 9 on page 127). As a city gardener, I'm a total fraud, and getting better at it every day!

Left: Under the dreamy eyes of a young romantic ($1 at a Copake Auction cleanout sale), from the left, a rose fabric lampshade studded with faded green pom-poms, 50 cents at a church rummage sale; a rose-crowned mirror, a gift from a London flea market; and a letter from Martha Stewart!
Preceding pages: A daybed tucked into a sunny corner thriving with flowers I'll never have to water! The best pillow contradicts a camp song my sisters and I used to sing called "Daisies Will Not Tell." I had to stretch for the quartet of paintings both physically (they were tucked away on top of a very high chest at Stan'z, Kingston, New York) and economically (after forgoing them twice I paid $200 for the lot).

The large embroidered flower on the face of what I refer to as the "Raggedy Ann" pillow creates a blooming nose and leafy grin. Before it was abandoned to the family warehouse—the barn at Muskettoe Pointe Farm—it cozied-up a guest house sofa, and can be revisited in *American Family Style* (Viking Studio Books, 1988) on page 112.

Stories of my mother's ingenuity are legend, but (as I've told before in *American Junk*, Viking Studio Books, 1994) I love her Christmas-in-the-Barn tradition. Such a large family (I think you know I'm the oldest of nine) collects stuff like crazy, filling up the attic, basement, and barn, at Muskettoe Pointe Farm. Every Christmas for the last several, each child and spouse draws a number and waits in line to pick a fanciful present (just about anything) from the barn. (The irony, so clever, is that we're slowly cleaning out each other's stuff!) This year I chose the ragtag pillow (opposite). It reminds me (I think it's the fringe) of the head of Raggedy Ann!

Left: The Chinese silk kimono, hanging nonchalantly off a door, was pulled out of a box at D's Place at Holland's Stage Coach Markets in Gloucester, Virginia, two days after Christmas 1995. It must have been 20 below in that shop, but the poor owner let me take a quick look. I think I bought the kimono as an extra layer for $8. (It didn't help!) I love old textiles (robes, blankets, fabrics, remnants) strewn around, hung, or stacked as pieces of textured, in this case, garden art.

Right: I've never been a curtain kind of person, but I loved the big roses blooming from this old pair found at the Second Chance shop in Southampton, New York. They were very heavy, and a little pricey, but when they blow in the breeze from the twelfth story of our city home I could swear I smell a rosy elixir!

Opposite: The skull has been a fixture in our city home for a decade. I was so in love with Georgia O'Keeffe (still am) at the time I discovered it hanging on the outside of Jerry Pontes's antiques shop in Kill Devil Hills, North Carolina, that I would have tied myself to his front door before I left without it. He was genuinely impressed, but never lets me forget how much he <u>didn't</u> want to give it up—for $25, I think. I'm not sure when the silk roses were added. But, the other day my older son, Carter, pointed out his favorite O'Keeffe—*Cow's Skull with Calico Roses*, 1931. It's pretty close.

The chandelier and the tulle prom dress strewn with flowers both remind me of wedding cakes—those mighty tiered towers glistening with shiny frosting and bedecked with a million pastel buds. The chandelier was swinging from a nail in a dark, junk-packed shed at Stan'z in Kingston, New York. The dress I have seen for several summers at The Twila Zone in Nags Head, North Carolina. Jo Ruth, the owner, always hangs it in a different spot. (Last summer it was on the front door.) I've never even asked the price it seems so much a part of the place. The chandelier I didn't hesitate to buy for $25. Now, it swings from a nail in my sun-filled Garden Hutte—the first blooming thing to take root.

Above: In the North they are called "snow" fences and hold back drifting snow. In the South, specifically on the Outer Banks of North Carolina, they are called "sand" fences and control drifting sand. Whatever you call them, these fences are simply four-foot pickets of spruce wired together. At Kitty Hawk Building Supply in Kitty Hawk, North Carolina, a fifty-foot roll—enough for you and a friend—costs $24.99. (Prices may vary.) They last forever and when they start to fade you can turn them upside down and make a sand fence arbor like Gilligan's, seen opposite and below.

1. Create an arc with a roll of sand fence (you'll need approximately 18 feet) using the doorway as your guide. Clip off excess fence with heavy wire clippers.

2. Starting from the top of the door, staple the bottom row of picket wire to the inside perimeter of the doorway so that the fence juts out perpendicular to the wall.

3. An old board stabilized on one side by the arbor becomes an instant plant stand. A weathered oar or extraneous piece of driftwood adds character and support.

f you ran into the little shack on the preceding pages, you'd probably give a holler, "Is there anybody home?" And, upon receiving no answer (which is what you had expected), you might take a peek inside (well, there's no door, for starters!). No, this is not the story of Goldilocks, and certainly this is not a cave for three bears. You tiptoe in under a tropical arbor dripping with vines (what is it made of?). There's a sandy floor, tie-dyed surfer jams, Hawaiian shirts, an old guitar, shells piled into plant stands, plants piled into bright straw beach hats, barnacles, and buoys. A little sign outside reads—"The Down Under." Is this the outpost of an Australian surfer? No, wait a minute, now you've got it! It's not Fantasy Island, but yes, of course, it's Gilligan's Island! Yes, Gilligan could definitely live here. After the TV series went into reruns, the Captain, the Professor, Mr. and Mrs. Howell, Ginger, and Mary Ann sailed back to their former lives, but Gilligan stayed behind to plant a garden that grows outside and inside his beach garden shanty. Herewith, lighthearted inspiration for paradise getaways and gardens of our own.

Left: The sand fence arbor in place and blooming with twirling grapevines and the bright red fuzzy blooms of a castor bean plant. Other quick-fix trellis and arbor growers: morning glories (the fastest and most adaptable), clematis, wisteria, and good old honeysuckle. (Roses take real commitment, but boy, are they worth it!)

Left: Softwear for a deep red-leaved *Caladium*—a seafoam-green canvas water bucket. The last thing Gilligan grabbed when the boat went down! The splotchy green trowel was 50 cents from Hot Line, Too in Kill Devil Hills, North Carolina.

Opposite: Blooming from the tropical trellis created by layering leftover sand fence pickets on top of the existing horizontal boards are, clockwise from left: a straw fish for 75 cents from the Teen Challenge Thrift Store, Kill Devil Hills; a barnacled buoy brought in with the tide; a 50-cent basket of shells from Hot Line Thrift Shop in Manteo; a black crow silhouette made by Maurice from Duck, North Carolina; a newspaper cap (at bottom), $1, and yellow-handled clippers (just above), $2, from Bermuda Triangle, Nags Head. (All towns of the Outer Banks of North Carolina.)

133

a tailgate picnic for junk lovers

Adding personality to a summer getaway, even if it's just for a week, is, in my mind, totally essential. Save the hunt for a rainy day and if, at the end of your holiday, you don't want to drag everything home (never entered my mind!), donate it back to the thrift shops you bought it from. Most of those we hit in the Outer Banks, like Teen Challenge, which supplied our tailgate spread (above) and the whimsy to Gilligan's getaway, are dedicated to good causes.

1 tie-dyed surfer jams	$2.00
2 bandannas	.50
1 blue basket	.75
1 straw fish	.75
1 sunflower print shirt	$2.50
1 3-D straw flower masterpiece	.75
1 blue Hawaiian shirt	1.00
1 American flag and flagpole	1.00
2 *Reader's Digest* compilations	.50
Grand Total	**$10.25**

Right: A blazing sunset spotlights the back wall of Gilligan's sandy-floored retreat. His mix of hangups is a good lesson in anything goes in the good old summertime. Tie-dyed jams hung on the wall? Pop Art for $2!

Opposite: 1. A spiffy straw Bermuda basket, $10, from The Twila Zone, Nags Head. **2.** A woman with flowers on the brain—a decoupaged hat form, $5, from Hot Line Thrift, Manteo. **3.** A straw hat relic that looks as if it narrowly escaped the sequined net that covers it—25 cents from Charles Reber in Nags Head. **4.** The handcrafted table was $20, by Jerry Pontes of Pontes Antiques, Kill Devil Hills. Atop the table, a pair of hat basket plant holders, painted bright yellow, which cost 25 cents each at Merry-Go-Round Thrift Shop in Kill Devil Hills. The big straw fan on the wall in the upper right was one of a pair for 75 cents at Hot Line Thrift Shop, Manteo. **5.** The tie-dyed jams were $2. **6.** The unfinished lighthouse painting is by Jerry Pontes of Pontes Antiques. **7.** The straw flower art, 75 cents. **8.** The four-foot metal plant stand of conchs was $6 from Pontes Antiques in Kill Devil Hills.

How can you not like a thrift shop with an ocean view and a dog named Radar to welcome you at the door? Those are just two good things about Kitty Hawk Thrift, Consignment & Antiques, Kitty Hawk, North Carolina. The third, fourth, and fifth are the three pieces of wicker garden furniture seen above. They were right out front catching those ocean breezes and costing me $40.

I recently discovered a Matisse I'd never seen before entitled *Tea (Le Thé)*. It is a large (55 by 83 inches) garden composition (see my brother Jimmie's interpretation on page viii) painted in the summer of 1919, in Issy-les-Moulineaux, France. Two women are seated casually in pale green garden chairs near a tall round table laid out with a tea urn, a blue-and-white ceramic pitcher, linen napkins, and scattered lemons and limes. One woman is Matisse's daughter Marguerite. In the foreground, scratching very intently, is a funny gray dog. Gilligan's wicker garden party, set up in his tropical backyard (seen on the preceding pages and opposite), is light-years away from the tea party at Issy, and yet there is something about the placement of the table and chairs, the pastel bandannas, the lavender lily-of-the-valley pillow, and the funny watercolored *Reader's Digest* book covers that takes me there. Imagine Gilligan inviting Marguerite and her friend, dressed in their dainty flowered frocks and little high heels, to join him in his garden for, not tea, but tumblers of cool rum punch! Their dog would probably not be able to travel (there's quarantines to think about), so Gilligan rings up his friends at Kitty Hawk Thrift, Consignment & Antiques (where the wicker furniture came from) and invites Radar, who looks a little like the dog in Matisse's painting, to join them. There you have it. A very mad tea party inspired by a French Impressionist's garden masterpiece and ship-wrecked Gilligan's garden junk!

Above: An underwater garden surveyed by a trio of sea horses from the cover of a water-stained *Reader's Digest Condensed Book* from spring 1962, a first edition for 25 cents, from the $10 haul made at Teen Challenge Thrift Shop in Kill Devil Hills, North Carolina. The turquoise starfish necklace beside it could be a mermaid's garland plucked from the same undersea book cover. It was, in fact, plucked from Kitty Hawk Thrift, Consignment & Antiques, in Kitty Hawk for $14.

Left: A she-sells-seashells kind of basket (75 cents from Teen Challenge), spray-painted a deep sea blue and layered with bleached-out clam shells. They remind me of Georgia O'Keeffe's collection of bone fragments—her flowers of the desert.

Opposite: Twenty-five-cent bandannas the color of summer ices serve as instant summer upholstery tucked around the cushions of the wicker chairs also seen on the preceding pages. Another *Reader's Digest* first edition, autumn 1961, is a seaweed sister to the one above. Same price—a quarter! The straw hat, above it (is it Gilligan's or Marguerite's?) was $1, at the Hot Line Thrift Shop in Kill Devil Hills. You can almost smell the lilies-of-the-valley blooming out of the deep purple landscape of the little throw pillow found at Bermuda Triangle for $4.50, in Nags Head, North Carolina.

from
arles with love

Above, left and right: Sunrise and Sunset, the name of this sunflower variety, is reflected in its golden and dark rich shades. They are arranged in a tall red vase picked up at least five years ago for $8 at a flea market (readers of *American Junk*, now in paperback, Penguin Studio Books, $19.95, will remember it from page 2) and placed on a simple wooden table. I think of van Gogh in his stark little bedroom in Arles arranging his own sunflowers like those he painted at right (*Still Life with Fourteen Sunflowers*, Arles, August 1888) featured on the cover of an exhibition catalogue. These catalogues can be collected for as little as $2.50, which is what I paid for this treasure, found in a huge stack at Rodgers Book Barn in Hillsdale, New York.

Above left: Appearing at The Hen Nest in Seminole, Florida—"The Sunflower Sisters," a trio of painted papier-mâché works of art looking as if any minute they might burst into song. Pass the microphone please! (See one of the three transplanted to New York City, page 179, $10 each.)

Above right: My good friend Elsie Albig, a neighbor in the country, had been struggling with how to create the center of a wooden sunflower she was potting when she spied a palm mat a little over 5 inches in diameter at a crafts store. Others might have seen a coaster, Elsie saw sunflower seeds. Her husband, Bob, carved the two layers of petals with a band saw, then tacked and glued them onto a 3/8-inch dowel. Assembled and painted by Elsie, the sunflower went—squish—into a block of florist Styrofoam secured in a clay pot and bedded over with Spanish moss. Lately, a perky black crow has come to roost.

Opposite: After the beanstalk climb, Jack might have tackled this sturdy sunflower, crafted of wood by Florida artist Al Raun. It stands about five feet in the shade of a litchi nut tree outside The Garden Room at Provence, a fertile paradise for collectors, located in Belleair Bluffs, Florida. It comes apart and costs about $125.

Left: Closer inspection of Al Raun's handmade sunflower reveals a few rough spots. Judy Shoup, chief gardener of The Garden Room, displays it indoors and out. "Not that it needs sun or rain to nourish it, but I love it in both environments, and the weathering gives it even more character."

Above: My sunflower perch seen through a window of my Garden Hutte.

sunflower perk— a perch!

My neighbors Bob and Elsie are like those good elves who finish the cobbler's work after he or she has fallen asleep! Every weekend when I finally arrive at the farm and make my way as quickly as possible to the Garden Hutte, there is usually some hint of their handiwork. Besides watering my plants, which they do faithfully, frequently a surprise awaits. A really charming one came at the end of last summer—an amazing sunflower perch on which roosted a very contented crow. Here's how to make your own.

Obtain a mammoth sunflower (beg, borrow, or grow!), then dry it, which you can do by hanging the flower upside down in a dry, protected place. When dry, trim off the stalk and place the sunflower, seeds up, in a sling constructed of four pieces of raffia (Elsie's pieces were about a yard long), knotted at the bottom and top. It's pretty if you allow for some extra raffia fringe underneath. Hang your perch outdoors and you may find real birds stopping by for a quick treat. To promote a longer life find a home inside in a porch, sunroom, or sunny kitchen window.

Above: In midsummer my son Carter returned from a trip to a nearby town with three baby sunflower plants. They were the first initiates planted in our new ground and Carter's first real attempt at gardening since he was six. They were a hearty group and with Carter's weeding, watering, and worrying they grew to a height of three feet with many, many blossoms. Most of these we dried and stuck on the Hutte's bulletin board (see page 23) and into a large bouquet that hangs over the mantelpiece next to Monsieur Armand Roulin (see inside front or back cover).

Above: Swap shops, junk yards, and yard sales are great providers of utility garden aids. The collection of next-to-new seed spreaders at A-Z Swap, Clearwater, Florida, testifies to this notion. Average price: $10.

Left: Garden spreaders distribute, so I've read, grass seed, lawn food, and the like in an even and speedy fashion. Intrigued, I invested $3 in a rusty blue Ward's Garden Mark model showcased quite graphically in front of a poppy-colored circular table top at Stan'z Used Items & Antiques, Kingston, New York. I've yet to yard-test it, but I'm confidently prepared for next year's lawn.

Opposite page: Guess what this green wheeled thing is and, well, you could win it! Clue: It was manufactured by the American Lawn Mower Company. Clue: Located in Muncie, Indiana. Clue: It has a small wooden roller like a push mower. It also has rotating clippers like a mower. Time's up! No clue? My guess: It's a mini-mower and edger for hard-to-cut places like flower borders. I should know since I bought it for $10, at a yard sale at Northeast Antiques, Millerton, New York. If you have a better idea, write me c/o Penguin Studio, Penguin USA, 375 Hudson Street, New York, NY 10014, and just maybe I'll send it to you!

Above and opposite page: It stole my heart, this little orphaned pedal tractor totally rusted-out and forsaken at Stan'z, Kingston, New York, for $30. I had a vision of a home for it in the Garden Hutte yard (see it there on page 25), a little piece of childhood sculpture to be nurtured by visiting children, romping dogs, and lots of growing weeds and flowers.

For my last birthday some friends surprised me with a Garden Junk party. The main centerpiece of the table was a perfect child-sized John Deere tractor. Gasping with pleasure I was quickly informed that it was the boyhood treasure of the husband of one of the partygivers: I would <u>not</u> be riding it home. That tractor inspired the purchase of the one seen on the opposite page and above, and the little wheelbarrow at left. Children's garden tools and transportation are new toys in the hands of gardeners. Indoors or outdoors they make the most fetching garden decor, but unfortunately are fetching just as high prices. (I just passed up a 1950s rake, hoe, and spade set for $50!) Condition obviously plays a role, which is why my collection has a common patina—rust.

Left: A companion to the toy tractor seen opposite, a child's first wheelbarrow exhibited as nostalgic garden sculpture on a little lawn table outside the Garden Hutte. Collected for $3 at the Copake Country Auction Memorial Day flea market, Copake, New York. See its versatility demonstrated <u>inside</u> the Garden Hutte, on page 21.

"An unmowed lawn looks as bad as a man without a shave," points out a 1947 gardening guide. The tool of choice to keep things trim was the classic push mower (see pages 166–167), around since the 1800s. Imagine life before their gas-guzzling cousins. How quiet a Saturday in the American backyard must have been! The fifties changed all that. Today, we don't even push, we ride.

Opposite page: The best of all machines—it's silent, unless you count the "chug-a-chug" sounds made by a two-year-old. It's environmentally correct. It's lightweight. It provides exercise and all kinds of fun for anyone under three feet tall. Of course, there are taller exceptions, like you and me, who would see it as a perfect grown-up's toy to hang on a garden shed wall or park in an apartment twelve stories up next to a crazy-colored Adirondack chair. (Yes, I've done it all! See page 179.) Bought on the spot from the backyard grass of The Garden Room at Provence, Belleair Bluffs, Florida, for $22.

Top left: Dinosaurs of the garden-tech revolution—push power mowers abandoned with other outmoded forms of transportation at J's Odds & Ends, Largo, Florida. Unless you're looking for backyard architecture, you might want to pass the secondhand trail here. (The only time I've given this advice!)

Bottom left: Charles Reber, a resident of the Outer Banks of North Carolina and one of its most notable wood-carving artists, turned his talents to another medium when he took on the paint job of his shiny red power machine. It is <u>truly</u> a work of art, and "<u>Yes</u>," it works!

John Halpern was born into a family of artists, which might explain, he thinks, his strange passion for turning sixty-year-old-plus push mowers into representational art. In 1992, he bought an old turkey farm in Bridgehampton, New York. The barn, out back, seen at left, was "half fallen down." Four years ago he decided to save it. In the detritus of stuff he hauled out of it to the dump was an old push mower. That night he had a dream about it. "I went back the next morning and retrieved it." The rest is "art history."

Today there are over sixty vintage push mowers in John's studio barn. He deconstructs them, sandblasts the parts, puts them back together, sprays them with clear lacquer, then stains the wooden handles. Connecting latex representations of the human form (hands and face) is where his art comes in. He casts not only his own face and hands, but those of his best friends and of acquaintances. After the casts are made, he carves out details, paints them, and affixes them to a wall—the faces above the hands, the hands attached to the handles of the mower. See an exemplary self-portrait installed in his Bridgehampton house, above right.

Above: The portrait of the artist (John Halpern) as a mower man. His latex face and hands clutch one of his sixty plus vintage mowers.

push the limit
lawn mower art

The push mower was created by the English—not to cut grass (sheep and scythes took care of that), but to trim the nap of carpets. John Halpern, an artist passionate about transforming mowers into one-of-a-kind working artworks, swears by their indestructibility. Models like "the New Favorite," made in America since the turn of the century by the American Lawn Mower Company in Muncie, Indiana, boasted self-sharpening, self-adjusting, and ball-bearing systems. Which is why, according to John, there are still so many in circulation. His average bargaining price–$10. My personal favorite, seen on page xii, snagged at a yard sale for $5, stands like a piece of rusty sculpture outside the Garden Hutte. Though I can appreciate a push mower as art, I appreciate it more when it artfully cuts the high grass in my Garden Hutte yard. If you're of the same mind, see general tool rehab tips on page 31.

All it took was the discovery of one old broken-down push mower in the turkey barn/studio to hook John Halpern. His one has turned into over sixty, a sampling of which is seen here. Average price: $10.

old paint

Most people roaming through the snowy backyard of Stan'z Used Items & Antiques in Kingston, New York, on the bleak January afternoon that I spotted the rusty green metal lawn chair, seen at left, might have seen an opportunity to strip it down, repaint it, and place it—good as new—in their summer yards. I saw it as an already perfect piece of green metal sculpture to add to a growing collection of outdoor furniture and artifacts moved indoors into our city (see page 179) and country (see page 176) abodes. This penchant for flip-flopping things meant for the outdoors to the indoors is a family trait. I never thought it remarkable or strange the end of that summer—years ago—when my parents asked my brothers and sisters and me to carry our old wooden picnic table inside to the kitchen. It was solid, and there was always room for an extra person or two to squeeze together on those long benches. Its old weathered boards—never painted—brought the easiness of outdoor living indoors—right through the winter. It never went back.

The choice to reform an old rusty lawn chair or table, to enjoy it outdoors in spring and summer, or to serve dinner around it in front of the fire, the way we do (see page 176) is totally personal. The good news is there's an endless supply of secondhand lawn furniture to be had for so little. All those backyards ("roofless rooms" the Victorians called them) from the Industrial Revolution to the fifties and sixties filled to the brim with cast iron, wicker, Adirondack wood, and mass-produced tubular metal lawn sets are now the bargain fodder of every roadside yard and tag sale, flea market, and heavenly salvage places like Stan'z, where this tale began. I did not buy the green chair that day, and though I still regret it, I have made up for it a hundredfold, as you will see by turning the pages of this chapter.

Opposite: Whether king or queen (do chairs have a gender?) of the mountain of junk, found at Stan'z Used Items & Antiques in Kingston, New York, this old (circa 1950) green tubular metal lawn chair has endured a licking from its stay in at least a hundred backyards. Getting it back to mint condition would take real commitment (see page 174 to see if you have what it takes). My choice: Leave it to nature or invest the $10, bring it inside, and call it garden sculpture.

Above: A junk-yard lawn party at Stan'z in Kingston, New York, featuring a set of four 1940s lawn chair classics and a round table complete with fringed umbrella for $100.

Left: I overpaid by about $30 for this 1950s umbrella-stand lawn table—<u>without</u> the umbrella! The thin metal top is flimsily balanced on a separate leg base. What made me do it to the tune of $40? I loved the dismantled layers of red and green paint. Now officially retired from outside duty, it displays some of my favorite flower pots and vases in the Garden Hutte (see a peek of it through the doorway, on page 13).

A drive-by sighting of six backyard veteran lawn chairs, in the front yard of the Amenia Auction Gallery in Amenia, New York, left the impression of a slightly out-of-step chorus line. I turned around, of course, and went straight back for a closer look. The deal was $75 for the set. I chose two of the more distinguished for $20 apiece. (See them in their new home on pages 24 and 25.) The pinwheel cutouts in their backs and their weathered-out rusty shades of red and green elevated them, in my mind, to almost folk art status.

old paint
(take it off,
take it all off!)

I love the look of old paint (on wood and metal), but if chipping paint and corrosive rust aggravate you, here are some hints from people I trust.

There are two ways to remove old paint—by hand (very tedious!) or with chemical strippers. Zip-Strip and Rock Miracle are two of the strongest and best known. A water-based stripper, 3M Safest Stripper, is less toxic, but takes longer to do the job. Proceed with caution, paying strict attention to the directions on the package. Work outdoors when possible or in a well-ventilated space, and wear a respirator and gloves.

Smaller jobs can be accomplished with a wire brush or by attaching a wire wheel to a drill. A little paint thinner on steel wool will remove small specks of paint. Always wear goggles.

After the stripping process, wash your furniture with soap and water, and let it dry completely. Raw steel can be sealed with polyurethane or lacquer. If you choose to repaint, start with a primer made for metal. They are usually red or gray, containing zinc oxide to prevent rust. When the primer dries, apply a durable oil-based outdoor paint.

If rust is the main culprit, use a little paint thinner on steel wool. For a really big job, Honey Wolters of Ruby Beets in Bridgehampton, New York—a great resource for restored and "as-is" old metal lawn furniture—recommends Rust Reformer. "It's like liquid Ajax. You put it on and it totally changes the consistency of the rust, so you can paint right over it or leave it as is!"

After dragging their heavy cast-iron furniture from place to place, what a blessed relief it must have been for the American backyard owner of the 1940s to indulge in the new variety of tubular steel lawn chairs. Their novel spring-back design afforded a modicum of comfort, their bright colors were cheering, and, best of all, their lightness (compared to their predecessors') offered a modern portability and major back-pain reduction. Souvenirs of those glory days fill these two pages.

Above: To nurture love and togetherness in the outdoors—a pair of two-seaters spotted in front of Holland's Stage Coach Markets in Gloucester, Virginia.
Left: A hapless weather-afflicted chair for sale outside U-Name-It in Watkins Glen, New York, appears to have been treated with dabs of pink calamine lotion—$32.
Opposite: 1. What does that sticker on the back of this turquoise beauty—just yards from the deep blue ocean in Nags Head, North Carolina—say? My guess—$15. Stop by The Twila Zone and find out for yourself. **2.** A small battalion of tubular and sheet steel lawn chairs decked out in camouflage green paint and rust from Copake Country Auction, Copake, New York, $10 each. **3.** The scalloped-back blue for $10, I left behind at D's Place in Gloucester, Virginia, because: a. It was the bitterest day of a bitter December; b. I was convinced at the moment that spring would never come; and c. The car was already full. Spring did come, the car is never full enough, and let's face it, I was a fool. **4.** An offshoot of metal mania—a tall, skinny stool picked up for $12 at the Amenia Auction Gallery in Amenia, New York.

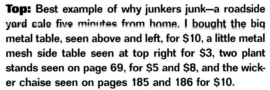

Top: Best example of why junkers junk—a roadside yard sale five minutes from home. I bought the big metal table, seen above and left, for $10, a little metal mesh side table seen at top right for $3, two plant stands seen on page 69, for $5 and $8, and the wicker chaise seen on pages 185 and 186 for $10.

Left: To welcome a garden table to a new life <u>inside</u> Elm Glen Farm, some garden touches—a scrawny herb in a blue glazed pot—$3 at Bottle Shop Antiques in Washington Hollow, New York; a plate of wooden apples from Hong Kong; a tulip-shaped wooden candleholder from a flea market in Paris; "The Temptation of Adam" in the open book and a glass of wine—for Eve and me.

new paint

The real scoop on how to make over flaking and rusting metal furniture is boxed on page 174. This is about faking it—finding something you can't live without and restoring it within an hour of getting it home, so that you can bring it right into your life <u>instantly</u>!

My heart's desire—the table seen at the yard sale, top left, had a pretty flimsy metal top, a hole for an umbrella, but no umbrella, and a substantial patina of rust and flaking paint. The filigreed double base made the sale. Here's what I did for love.

1. Paid $10. Got said object home as quickly as possible. Scraped off loose rust and paint with a large piece of fine steel wool.
2. Swished some pale green flat latex exterior paint with lots of water, making it into a lime-colored watercolor seen in the plastic cup on the little mesh table, top right, which also got a dose of it!
3. Soaked a large natural sea sponge into the wash and swirled it over the entire table. The results, seen at left and opposite, a lime-stained, almost translucent glow.
4. Let it dry for five minutes. Moved it into our country dining room. Set it with herbs, art books, a plate of wooden apples, three French café chairs, and a glass of white wine.
5. Q. Did I know exactly how this would turn out? A. No! Q. Am I happy? A. Beyond, beyond!

Opposite: If you're concerned about wooden furniture rotting away in the outdoors, then bring it inside! My Adirondack chair-of-many-colors, found at the bottom of a heap of old furniture in a secondhand shop on the Outer Banks of North Carolina for $20, has thrived under a ficus tree in our New York City living room. It came exactly as is—someone else's restoration project-in-process. I loved it, and named it "The Jasper Johns Chair," because it looked like a chair he might have loved and painted.

Above: First, you have to accept the fact that collecting—like anything that brings pleasure—can become an addiction. Knowing that, one has to prepare for the endless and eventual confrontation with great bargains that can seize the mind and fog all clear thinking. A case in point, my bench above. I was lured to it at a large outdoor tag sale. It was marked $15. If I had been attracted to just the one, that would have been normal and acceptable. The problem was it was one of three (see them at the sale on page 180). Like penny candy, I wanted a handful—particularly when the seller told me I could have all three for $40. I now possess (am possessed by) three benches. Regrets? I have none.

178

Above: Roy Austin was drunk when he returned from World War II to his home in Cape Hatteras, North Carolina. He never sobered up and eventually became a legendary character of Hatteras. Jerry Pontes, a fisherman, artist, craftsman, collector, and owner of Pontes Antiques in Kill Devil Hills, North Carolina, often visited him in his tumbled-down Hatteras shack. One day Roy gave him the old driftwood bench seen above, which now sits outside Jerry's home and gallery shop. Jerry inscribed it in blue paint with a sentiment he'd heard from an old seafaring hymn—"I'll anchor my suol (he admits to misspelling soul!) in a haven of rest and sail the seas no more."

Opposite, clockwise from top left: 1. Jerry Pontes only collects benches with character that were owned by characters that he knew. Like the one Roy Austin gave him, above, and this one, which he refers to as Mrs. Dowdy's bench. "When she moved," Jerry reports, "I helped her out and she gave it to me." **2.** My neighbor Kitty Paris has dotted the hilly landscape of her country retreat with vintage flowers <u>and</u> benches. Her wooden slatted curved-back bench, on an iron base, reminiscent of a nineteenth-century European park bench, was $40 from <u>our</u> favorite resource for that sort-of-kind-of-thing— Stan'z in Kingston, New York. **3.** In her last summer cottage in Sag Harbor, New York, Ellen O'Neill's little Adirondack-style bench from the forties sat smack-dab in the middle of the downstairs sitting room. (If you read *American Junk*, you saw it on page 221.) When Ellen moved to a new house, only minutes away, the bench came too, but in its new life it has been returned to the outdoors. **4.** If I had to park myself on a bench for eternity, this would be the one—a little wooden slatted school bench with cast-iron sides outside Rodgers Book Barn in Hillsdale, New York. **5.** If a bench could talk, this one, in front of Jerry Pontes Antiques, would have its own talk show. According to Jerry, it used to sit in front of the old fishing plant in Cape Hatteras. Some of the bench has signs of whittling. Jerry got it after the old plant was torn down. **6.** The three benches I seized on at Copake's annual Memorial Day tag sale that taught me a lesson (revealed on the preceding pages) of how-to-confront-a-bargain-that-you-don't-need-in-your-life-and-walk-away-from-it (well, sort of taught me!) were $40.

Above left: Though the leaves indicate fall, I remember with certainty it was January when I dug up this what looks like a skeleton of an old wrought-iron garden chair (and its mate) for $50 at Stan'z in Kingston, New York. Both hibernated for the winter in our barn and in spring found a home and homegrown seats (see them on pages 202–203).

Above right: Wrought iron has a wonderful flexibility clearly demonstrated by the twirly intricacies of the back of what I call my tulip chair—another of a pair picked up on that cold January hunt at Stan'z. Its missing seat was eventually replaced and softened with a dime-store pillow and a swatch of flowers stolen from some remnant yardage.

Above left: Cast iron has endured from the gardens of the Victorian Age until today where archetypal pieces can be found in the front yards of auction houses like the Amenia Auction Gallery in Amenia, New York, where this stalwart chair stood. Though it resembles its later wrought-iron cousins, it was cast in sand (whence its name) and built solidly to last—not to move.

Above right: Though wrought-iron chairs are sensible for life in the outdoors, and some like the one above on exhibition at the Amenia Auction Gallery in Amenia, New York, appear as delicate as lace, one thing they are <u>not</u> is comfortable. So, buy them for their beauty and sensibility, and let your plants sit in them!

Above: Dressed in tie-dyed jams I engaged in a different technique for turning my floor a mossy hue. **Left:** Watered-down paint, gloves, and a sea sponge are all it takes.

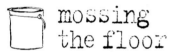

mossing the floor

After the concrete floor of the back half of the Garden Hutte courtyard (see page 186 for a fuller view) was poured and set, I became obsessed and impatient with a vision of it stained an organic mossy green. I knew in time it would reach that state naturally, but as usual, I couldn't wait.

Pour an inch or two of velvet flat 100% acrylic latex paint (pale green) into a plastic bucket and add a cup or two of water to create a water-colory wash. After sweeping all debris off the concrete, I dipped a large natural sponge into the mixture and without squeezing it out applied puddles of the wash to the floor in large sweeping strokes.

The concrete, being so porous, gulps in the liquid almost instantly. You can see within minutes the spots you missed or decide if you want to layer on more color. I found some areas soak in more color than others. I liked that patchy look—like the real thing.

I debated endlessly over what to do with the floor under the back half of the open shed attached to the Garden Hutte on the western side (see floorplan on page 11, and the photograph on page 10). I wanted something a little more solid than the rocky patio I had laid in front of it, and something cleaner than the original dirt floor. I loved the concrete floor (with all its cracks) that had been poured years before in the Garden Hutte, so I decided to go for the same effect. Joseph Zullo, my Garden Hutte technical adviser, oversaw the pouring of the 4-inch-deep, 12 by 21-foot area with 3,000 pounds of floor mix. The cost: $275. It took a day to dry, and then my dream of mossy finish for it took hold. (See the box opposite for how I faked it, and the results on the following spread).

Clockwise from top left: 1. A man named Travis sold me this fine, slightly deteriorating wicker chaise for $10, from his frontyard tag sale last Labor Day weekend in Millerton, New York. I should have stopped there. I didn't. For more of what I couldn't leave behind, see page 177. **2.** Work gloves transformed into garden sculpture by layers of dirt and green paint from my mossing escapade. **3.** A gift with my purchases from Travis, my tag sale friend in Millerton—a wobbly wooden seater almost restored to its natural unpainted state through benign neglect. **4.** You heard of Jerry Pontes's love of wooden benches (on page 181). This doesn't exclude a love of wooden tables. This one (seen previously on page 21) he made himself and sold to me for $25 as a platform for plants and artistic endeavors (seen opposite and on pages 186–87).

On a carpet of mossy watercolored concrete, a peaceful corner offering relief from the sun on a gardener's kind of La-Z-Boy—a wicker chaise (the one found at Travis's yard sale for $10) strewn with the flowers of an old linen tablecloth found in mint condition at Northeast Antiques, Millerton, New York, $15. The little metal side table (seen previously on page 177) displays paint-by-number ballerinas, $2; an urnlike vase spattered with soft shades of lavender from Bottle Shop Antiques in Washington Hollow, New York, for $3.

Jerry Pontes's table is home to an ornamental cabbage in an embossed clay pot ($2.50), stalks of marble grapes in a colander ($3), and a still life of lilacs (50 cents). A straw laundry basket ($1) of dried-out grapevines is stored underneath. Travis's gift awaits a fugitive artist. Witness its new life in my Garden Hutte on the opposite page and the preceding ones.

187

garden bones

y evaluation of whether something has worth is pretty much predicated on what it's worth to me. Take the blue wire garden gate, seen at left and up close on the preceding pages. I spotted it and a mate hanging on a wall at an auction preview one Saturday afternoon. I hadn't come looking for gates, but with plans to fence in a little yard in front of the Garden Hutte I knew that I would need them, and I knew with certainty that these were the ones. Gates and fences, trellises and arbors are the skeletons of our gardens. They define, punctuate, and support the individual character of each vine and flower. In their prime, they disappear clothed in climbing roses, vines of honeysuckle, wisteria, grape, clematis, sweet peas, nasturtiums, morning glories, trumpet flowers, jasmine, and creeping vegetables. In the winter the weathered bones of wooden pickets, latticed twigs, trellises, arched arbors, wire borders, rocks, and stones define more vividly the stark borders of our sleeping land.

Left: Garden Hutte pup pals, Bo and Charley, enjoy the view through one of the two garden gates successfully bid on for $100, at the Copake Country Auction, Copake, New York. They were pulled out of an old barn in Montreal. Paging through an old Montgomery Ward 1957 *Farm Book* catalogue I found out more. They were known as Picket Style Walk Gates, woven wire pickets set in a galvanized steel pipe frame. In 1957, they cost about $11.50. The picket fence, new a year ago, cost $13 per panel (41 by 28 inches)—available at most building supply places.
Preceding pages: A close-up of my blue painted garden gate. The ornamental curlicue on top is the best thing about it.

191

 # gate keepers
(some tips for the hunt!)

There seems to be a new hunger for hunting down unusual gates, not just as a portal way into a country garden but also as an offbeat wall hanging in a city apartment. The likeliest of sources are salvage yards whose stock and trade is disassembled houses. (See the Junk Guide and check your local Yellow Pages.)

In a *Better Homes and Gardens Gardening Guide,* published in 1947, the editors recommend seven qualities of a good gate. They weren't, of course, suggesting you look for a used one, but these tips are still worth considering, _and_ rejecting! (The parenthetical comments are mine!)

1. Is at least 3 feet wide. (Keep in mind you may need one entrance big enough to accommodate a tractor mower or truck full of junk!)

2. Is well-braced against sagging. (But, I _love_ sagging!)

3. Latches easily. (I use a piece of looped twine to keep mine closed.)

4. Has rustproof hardware. (I failed here!)

5. Is designed for a degree of privacy. (If that's what you want!)

6. Doesn't squeak. (W-D 40 could help you out here, but sometimes a squeaky gate announces a visitor!)

Left: A more contemporary and no-nonsense pair of wire mesh garden gates at the entrance to Bob and Elsie Albig's flower and vegetable garden in upstate New York. In lieu of latches, a trio of broken hockey sticks does the job. The board at the bottom prevents critters from climbing under!

Above: Biding its time at a yard sale on the Outer Banks of North Carolina, a derelict picket fence awaits a rose-covered cottage to make it a home-sweet-home.

The original picket fence made of chestnut that still borders the front entrance of Muskettoe Pointe Farm (see Dedication page), my family's home in the Tidewater region of Virginia, was a present to my parents from a dear friend, Robert Carter Ball, who saved it from a seventeenth-century plantation nearby. When other sections were added, like the one at left that encloses the riverfront gardens, my brother Bernard hand-split and shaped them out of oak. (No small task, but worth it.) A fence like this was what I had dreamed of to enclose the Garden Hutte. Maybe the day when my prepackaged pickets give up the ghost, I'll give my brother a call.

Right: The hand-split picket fence at Muskettoe Pointe Farm embraces rows of day lilies, stalks of fennel, purple loosestrife *(Lythrum)*, English box bushes, and a holly topiary in the far left corner. It forms a toothy trellis for creeping clematis.

Above: A homemade lattice-like trellis discovered in a shed behind the Amenia Auction Gallery in Amenia, New York. I was just pulling out when I spotted the trellis as you see it above. I begrudgingly paid $10 for it. (Too much! But it's earned its keep.)

Right: My trellis with its back against the wall of the Garden Hutte. Since the bottom stake was a little wobbly I nailed the whole trellis flat against the wall. A wild grapevine was growing nearby, so I pulled it over and let nature take its course.

Opposite page, left: Sometimes a trellis is a fence or a fence post. A few wooden rungs hammered at an angle to this shaped post, indigenous to those of eighteenth-century Tidewater, Virginia, acts as a stepladder to a wayward honeysuckle vine alongside the herb garden at Muskettoe Pointe Farm.

Opposite page, top right: An old stepladder leaning against the exterior of Retro, New Milford, Connecticut, could easily support clematis, sweet-smelling honeysuckle, climbing roses, grapevine, or wisteria. While you're waiting for your climbers to climb, you could let hanging pots of blooming annuals fill the space.

Opposite page, bottom right: A three-rung trellis stuck into the ground supports a wisteria bush in need of more sustenance than provided.

196

Above: A garden hitchhiker, a classic fan-shaped trellis, at a roadside tag sale in upstate New York. Note the missing spoke and rotting foot post. A handyman's special for $10.

Right: A gardener's legacy, old-fashioned red roses, passed along to us by Helen Hutchinson when we moved into Elm Glen Farm, her former home, in upstate New York. The concrete hen came from Williamsburg Pottery, Lightfoot, Virginia, for $10. The Adirondack chair picked up at a yard sale for $5, recently has been spiffed up with stripes of green and white paint.

Opposite page, top: Consider turning these two sections of wrought iron fence, circa 1950, vertically, attaching them to the side of a wall, and you have an imaginative habitat for roses, morning glories, scarlet runner beans, or clematis. For sale at a yard sale in upstate New York; I did not ask the price, but wager the owner would have been delighted to let me cart them off for less than $15.

Below, left and right: Hob Nail Antiques on Route 22, in Pawling, New York, appears to be a ghost town of old iron and brass beds. Scattered helter-skelter in front of the low white building, once a flower nursery, are thousands of gone-to-seed headboards, footboards, and side rails rusting and peeling old paint. One day, a couple of years ago, beckoned by the beauty of an extraordinary old iron bed set up right near the road, I pulled in for a closer look. My shock was walking inside Hob Nail and finding a total reversal of the exterior chaos. For every crumbling bed seen on the outside there was a fully restored, freshly painted or polished counterpart on the inside. Jerry Winrow, the owner, is the savior of these lost souls. That's the good news. The bad news is I wanted to take the bed as-is and "save" it myself! I envisioned an old headboard covered with flowering honeysuckle or grapevine—a sleeping-beauty kind of trellis. Unfortunately for me, Jerry only parts with beds he has born-again. My mission (and yours, if you're on the same track) is to seek out others.

When most people hear Watkins Glen, New York, they think of race cars. However, the main drag is not filled with race cars (though, of course, there is a famous race track nearby), but with collectibles shops. The Ballroom Co-Op at 315½ N. Franklin is upstairs. That's where I found the two miniature wooden trellises seen at left. I bought four for 50 cents each. It wasn't until much later, when I decided to try training some fledgling vines on them, that I discovered they were, in fact, miniature easels for displaying rare plates or small canvases like the roses painting they're leaning on. (Turn the book upside down and see them with three feet on the ground!) Oh, well, now I can use them all year round. The cast-iron floral fragment in the lower right (I sometimes use it as a romantic paperweight) probably came from the back of an ornamental garden bench. It was 50 cents at Antiques & Collectibles, Washington Hollow, New York.

stake your claim

If you don't run across your own set of tiny trellises (or easels!) you can stake your claim for growing tiny climbers by making a little wigwam of flexible cane sticks or rustic twigs entwined together and stuck in a small pot or urn. Jasmine, sweet pea, honeysuckle, clematis, even small roses will thrive happily on a patio or balcony given a little earth and a little urging.

garden sculpture

he enchantment of a garden comes sometimes from benign neglect. Turn back a page to the opening of this chapter and pause for a moment on an overgrown corner of the Garden Hutte yard furnished with a cement birdbath and two bottomless chairs. This is not a place for human repose. Even though the bottoms of the chairs are now cushioned with the feathery tufts of wild vegetation flowing under and around them, they offer repose only to our eyes. Gardens are prime gallery space for the most wide-ranging exhibits of garden sculpture. Whether it's classical urns or pink plastic flamingos, limestone saints or impish ceramic elves, Ionic Styrofoam pedestals or poured concrete birdbaths, <u>you</u> are the curator of your own backyard exhibition.

Preceding pages: A pair of wrought-iron chairs (seen before on page 182), whose backs resemble ancient lyres, were bought as is (no bottoms!) at Stan'z Used Items & Antiques, Kingston, New York, for $75. The birdbath dish incised in a classical halfshell and set on a fluted column is a concrete reproduction bought for $20 from a friend who was giving up her country garden for a loft in the city. **Left:** At Holland's Stage Coach Markets, Gloucester, Virginia, birdbaths—petaled and plain—garlanded urns, and our Lady, Mother of God, await greener pastures. Pottery like this is typical of mass-produced garden statuary made by pouring concrete into molds. (See page 206 for how to make it look centuries old!)

Above: Brand-new concrete garden sculpture exhibited in the dead of winter at Holland's Stage Coach Markets, Gloucester, Virginia. Birdbaths seem to be the item of the day, set on different-sized pedestals and plinths. Left out in the weather like this they will slowly start to age like the three seen at the right. To speed up the process, see the box below.

lichen or not ...
how to age garden artifacts

Manure and water is a tried-and-true way to get lichen, moss, and algae-related crusty stuff growing on surfaces. Cow or horse manure (the real thing is the best) can be bought in dehydrated form at a garden supplier. Mix it with a little water and apply with a sponge, rag, or brush.

I've been told by other creative agers that buttermilk and yogurt do an excellent job on cement and concrete garden ornaments. Dab on the buttermilk or yogurt with a sponge into the crevices and spots that would be the natural places for moss and lichen to grow. To speed up the process, rub a piece of sheet moss (available at most garden shops), or real moss (if you have it), into the areas where the mixture has been applied. This will introduce spores.

Seal the object in a garbage bag and bake in the sun for from one to three weeks. "Just keep checking on how things are growing," Judy suggests, "and be prepared for a lovely smell!"

If all of this sounds just a little too organic, you can wait for nature to take its course, or see the "mossing" with paint ideas on page 184.

Above: The moss-stained, scallop-like petals surrounding the pool of this birdbath, in the front yard of Provence Art & Antiques, Belleair Bluffs, Florida, is an example of the effect the aging recipes could achieve. The rough edges of the concrete base belie a masterpiece. Cathy Ottaviani, the owner of Provence, transported it from her own yard when the shop opened. For $75 you can move it to yours!

Above, left: A concrete birdbath from an old home in Tampa, Florida, circa 1950, is now the centerpiece of a butterfly garden outside The Garden Room at Provence, Belleair Bluffs, Florida. Judy Shoup, the garden's creator, shared with me why the stones are in the birdbath. "They're a landing pad for the butterflies nourished in our garden, which we planted solely to attract them and support each stage of their lives." The Garden Room at Provence specializes in butterfly gardens. For more information see the Junk Guide.

Above, right: A bird could drown in the depth of this pool, therefore I guess this isn't a birdbath, but a bowl-like urn attached to a pedestal. The rough edges of the concrete may be attributed to a mold that has not been well cleaned. T. S. Eliot wrote that "April is the cruelest month." In Virginia, which is where I spotted this sad little urn filled with dead leaves, January could be.

Clockwise from left: 1. From Twice Nice, New Milford, Connecticut, a birdbath with a pink-stained dish set on a fluted pedestal. It had been left behind by the owner's daughter months before. I begged him to sell it to me. Blood is thicker than water. **2.** In the back-yard of Pontes Antiques, Kill Devil Hills, North Carolina, an Ionic plaster pedestal, made in Mexico, is a strange side table to the wooden slatted chair beside it. It was one of six Jerry Pontes brought back five years ago from the Williamsburg Pottery, Lightfoot, Virginia, $25. **3.** Ellen O'Neill's birdbath, the centerpiece of her garden in Sag Harbor, New York (see number 12 on opposite page for another of its treasures) was a gift-with-purchase of the house. **4.** An English birdbath with a whimsical carved pedestal made of crushed stone, $50, on sale, at King William Antiques, Toano, Virginia. **5.** The little English bird-bath (seen in number 4, above) is the centerpiece of one of Muskettoe Pointe's riverfront gardens, blooming spring flowers. **6.** A heavy-duty cement pedestal with applied vines and flowers, set in front of the Garden Hutte windows (see picture 4 on page 11 for a fuller view). The stamens of the flower set on the plinth are made of galvanized nails. Found in the yard at Stan'z Used Items & Antiques, Kingston, New York, for $40. I've not yet found a top worthy of it.

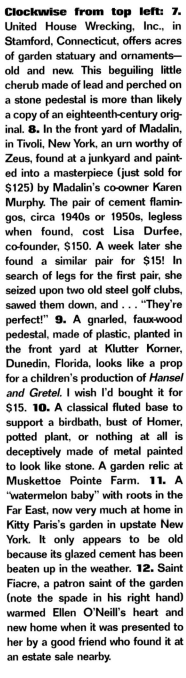

Clockwise from top left: 7. United House Wrecking, Inc., in Stamford, Connecticut, offers acres of garden statuary and ornaments—old and new. This beguiling little cherub made of lead and perched on a stone pedestal is more than likely a copy of an eighteenth-century original. **8.** In the front yard of Madalin, in Tivoli, New York, an urn worthy of Zeus, found at a junkyard and painted into a masterpiece (just sold for $125) by Madalin's co-owner Karen Murphy. The pair of cement flamingos, circa 1940s or 1950s, legless when found, cost Lisa Durfee, co-founder, $150. A week later she found a similar pair for $15! In search of legs for the first pair, she seized upon two old steel golf clubs, sawed them down, and . . . "They're perfect!" **9.** A gnarled, faux-wood pedestal, made of plastic, planted in the front yard at Klutter Korner, Dunedin, Florida, looks like a prop for a children's production of *Hansel and Gretel.* I wish I'd bought it for $15. **10.** A classical fluted base to support a birdbath, bust of Homer, potted plant, or nothing at all is deceptively made of metal painted to look like stone. A garden relic at Muskettoe Pointe Farm. **11.** A "watermelon baby" with roots in the Far East, now very much at home in Kitty Paris's garden in upstate New York. It only appears to be old because its glazed cement has been beaten up in the weather. **12.** Saint Fiacre, a patron saint of the garden (note the spade in his right hand) warmed Ellen O'Neill's heart and new home when it was presented to her by a good friend who found it at an estate sale nearby.

Above: The kitchen wing of Elm Glen Farm was the hub of the original house, built at the end of the eighteenth century.

The gently arched entryway into the kitchen at Elm Glen Farm, seen above, is my most-loved corner of the house. Shading it in spring and summer is a topiary-shaped lilac tree that blooms the most welcoming fragrance. Tucked in the base of its branches is a bird's nest, refurbished each spring by a new pair of tenants. Along the stone path and under the windows grows a thick green quilt patched with hostas, lily-of-the-valley, violets, periwinkle, and iris. To the left of the steps a little stone rabbit sticks out. Above him in the window box is a wily black crow. When the lilacs fade and the baby birds take flight, they'll stand their ground—the loyal garden centurions of my backdoor heaven.

Right: The silhouette of the black wooden crow stuck in the flower box, blooming pink impatiens and geraniums, was made recently by an artisan from North Carolina.

The little stone rabbit framed by hostas, bluebells, lily-of-the-valley, and periwinkle is a stone reproduction made by a Southern statuary company for about $50. I must sponge on some buttermilk or yogurt (see box on page 206) to speed up the mossing process.

According to Elsie Albig, the two little ceramic elves lolling by her miniature watering hole are the last of seven (Dwarfs!!). They were handcrafted by a local artisan, Betty Jenks, who had her kiln on nearby Winchell Mountain in upstate New York. "They've lived in my garden for over twenty-five years. Occasionally I do touch them up with a little acrylic paint," Elsie confesses.

Above: A precursor to Smurfs, this little plastic elf goes happily about his work wheeling a cargo of crab apples in his tiny barrow. Another Albig family elf!

As children, my brothers and sisters and I would plant fairy gardens in the crevices and hollows of tree stumps or nestled between the big raised roots in the woods near our home. At night we would creep to the edge of the woods and peer through the darkness looking for Tinkerbell's lights and the sound of tiny voices. In our imagination the elves and fairies inhabited not only the Enchanted Forest but also our gardens. They brought good luck and a magical tradition of wee garden folk (made of clay, cement, and plastic) to live happily ever after amid the sprawling, blooming vegetation of our seasonal labors.

Top left: Another Albig elf, not one of the original seven but older by about fifteen years, and made of cement, not clay. Elsie recently repainted his red hat.

Middle left: A German elf, "very grumpy," Elsie puts in, with a dirty beard and fingers curled into place where, once, a small wheelbarrow was secured.

Bottom left: A plaster elf pot for sale for $8 at an outdoor junkyard in upstate New York could use a little fix-up. Elsie suggests the two-ounce plastic bottles of acrylics, found in most crafts departments, manufactured by Delta or Deco Art.

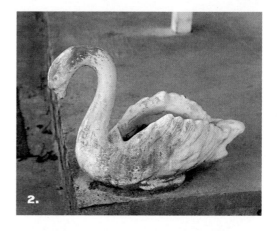

Clockwise from top left: 1. A little concrete hen, seen before in full on page 198, struts her stuff in wall-to-wall periwinkle growing over the concrete terrace just off the porch at Elm Glen Farm. It is from Williamsburg Pottery, Lightfoot, Virginia, $10. **2.** The ugly duckling grew up into a regal swan, but maybe not like this one—a little down on its luck, the feathered doorman outside a shop at Holland's Stage Coach Markets, Gloucester, Virginia. Scour the sides with a bristle brush, some warm soap and water, plant white petunias, and watch that regal head rise! **3.** Elsie Albig's Uncle Willy once had an amazing Japanese garden on a hillside overlooking a beautiful valley in northern Dutchess County, New York. The little stone dove, now perched in Elsie's garden, lived there once. Elsie believes he got it in Great Barrington, Massachusetts. It's molded cement, but whitened out by the weather so it looks almost like marble. **4.** The ceramic duck hidden under blooming branches, just outside the front door of the Albig home in Dutchess County, was made twenty years ago by Betty Jenks, the Winchell Mountain ceramicist who also created the two lolling elves seen back on pages 212-213.

Left: On a hillside in the southwestern part of New York State, where wild turkeys are a common sight, these four grazing pink flamingos take one's breath away! Which is exactly why Kitty Paris (see more on Kitty's garden surprises on pages 146 and 180), who found them stored in a neighbor's basement for a decade (they're thirty years old), put them there. Flamingos in the front yard are an American tradition of sorts. Forty years ago in Leominster, Massachusetts, Don Featherstone made a plastic version, and the lawn-ornaments company he worked for then (and still does), Union Products, started marketing them. They sell nearly a quarter million a year at about $9.95 to $12.95 a pair.

One of the good things about living in a large city, New York in particular, is the unexpected surprises to be found around each corner. I found two the first week we moved into our apartment almost twenty-five years ago. They're my street sisters, seen at left and opposite. Two exquisite sculpted goddesses that live in the ground floor courtyards of two elegant brownstones, one right across from the other. Every Christmas, a mysterious Santa places pine wreaths around their necks. It is a tradition, I discovered, that began over forty years ago. Every holiday season I wait for it to happen, and when it does I am filled with such hope, comfort, and joy.

Left: A French Aphrodite cast from a heavy metal, then painted, stands her ground on a delicate wave in the streetside courtyard of a New York brownstone. According to the owners, she has blessed their threshold for over forty years. She is hardly junk—her design has been attributed to the creator of Versailles.

Opposite: She may not look it, but this dainty limestone beauty that once graced the Art Nouveau facade (she was full figure then) of the old Ziegfeld Theatre at Fifty-fifth and Sixth, weighs in at about 4,000 pounds. Her owner for the last twenty-seven years tells how he was driving by the theater just before it was torn down with the man who was to accomplish that feat. He joked how he would love to have the sculpture as his own private muse (he being a writer for the theater and such!). A few months later he was startled by a huge commotion outside his brownstone. His muse had arrived unannounced—by crane. Her dignity and grace have remained intact despite the plastic garbage bins lined up beside her—beauty and necessity side by side.

217

view with a room

was with my friend Bruce Weber one day working on a photographic project on top of a mountain in some very beautiful place in Aspen, Colorado. It was snowing like crazy so we had taken a break for some hot chocolate, and I started to tell him about a little piece of land we had recently purchased overlooking the Rappahannock River, next to my family's home in Virginia. I was explaining the frustration of spending so little time there, and of not knowing when we would actually be able to live on it. Bruce suggested that we camp out on it—set up a tent, sleep under the stars, and take some kind of spiritual ownership of what was ours. We could also move the tent from place to place to find a perfect view. The following summer, seven years ago, we did just that. We put up a tent, not exactly what Bruce had in mind, but a raised wooden platform, seen at left (inspiration for how to create and embellish your own lies ahead on page 227). Four corner posts were attached at the top by a wooden railing so we could spread a canopy over it and fly the flag. (It was Fourth of July weekend.) My father and Benie Robins, a longtime friend of Muskettoe Pointe Farm and our family, served as the chief architect and builder. I helped choose the spot, then handed them nails and cold water.

At the end of the day, when the job was done, the three of us climbed up on the new structure and looked out at the three-mile-wide river and the sunset making the sky all pink and gold. I named it then "View with a Room," with special thanks to E. M. Forster, my father, and to Benie (who passed several months ago into that pink and gold Forever). That night at least a dozen of us, children of all ages, climbed up the crude cinder-block stairway to celebrate America's birthday under the starry sky. Amid the twinkling of a million lightning bugs, we watched a garden of flowery lights explode and grow over our heads, then rain into the silvery moonlit waters.

Opposite: 1. In the foreground a sawhorse props up several of the 10-foot by 1-inch by 6-inch salt-treated pine boards that will form the floor of the 10-foot square platform. My father, seen in the background to the left, points out how the boards should be positioned to Benie Robins, seen camouflaged behind a branch at right. (For directions on how to build your own "View with a Room" platform, see page 227.) **2.** The structure complete (it took a day), an American flag was attached to the front of the top rail and an old sheet was canopied over it all, readying the "View" as a viewing stand for the Fourth of July fireworks over the river. **3.** The platform was raised about 3 feet off the ground to allow for a better view of the river and to keep the undergrowth and small creatures at bay. **4.** My sister Emily, whose home is directly opposite our new residence—due south through a field of young pines and waist-high grass—pauses for a view of the "View" and another of the river just beyond the trees.
Preceding pages: View with a Room as it stands today, weathered a silvery gray and embellished with Victorian-shaped porch posts and spindle trim, transplanted from an 1890s farmhouse replete with miniature ghosts featured in *American Family Style* (Viking Studio Books, 1988, pages 40–45), and revisited just ahead on page 226.

On the seventh birthday of View with a Room, we decided to stage a romantic tableau, pulling props from the various dwellings of Muskettoe Pointe Farm. It shouldn't take long to guess the inspiration—the love story of the princess and the frog. (A sort of garden fable, I thought!)

Right: On the cinder-block steps of the palace, facing a money plant, a painted bird (a Mexican pottery piece on sale for $7 at the Williamsburg Pottery, Lightfoot, Virginia) guards the domain of the frog prince (a stone garden ornament, $18, at King William Antiques in Toano, Virginia) seen at right and on the opposite page. His dining table (a Victorian walnut side table with a shelf stretcher beneath, $35, from Cecil's Antiques in Richmond, Virginia), draped with a royal piece of green damask (a remnant my mother pulled off an old chair and couldn't part with), is decorated with royal pinecones and a centerpiece heirloom candelabra (maybe in fifty years!). The pair of carved chairs (two of ten my mother bought from a good friend almost thirty years ago for "a song," supposedly Chinese exports) is softened for the royal couple by matching pink velvet fringed pillows, $6 for the pair, from the Merry-Go-Round Thrift Shop, Kill Devil Hills, North Carolina. **Opposite, clockwise from top left: 1.** The "heirloom" candelabra was new four years ago and cost $18, from Ikea Washington, Woodbridge, Virginia. **2.** A cement urn filled with long stalks of purple lavender, from the Williamsburg Pottery, for a special price of $5. **3.** The miniature cement urn, almost like a goblet, was found along with the frog prince at King William Antiques, Toano, Virginia, for $14. The two brass goblets to the left of it, perfect for a royal aperitif, were $1 each at Penny Paid in Locust Hill, Virginia. **4.** The old picture frame hung pictureless in our barn for years. Perhaps it will soon frame the royal wedding portrait of the princess, seen just above it, and her soon-to-be-released-from-his-spell prince.

The frog prince has made his move, leaping over the table to the feet of his princess—an idealized young girl, probably Victorian, clothed in Grecian garb and crowned with an ivy wreath, set in a gold oval laid into a 14 by 9-inch gilt frame, from a group lot of pictures secured by my mother years ago at an auction in Norfolk, Virginia. Her stringed instrument appears to be a balalaika.

Opposite: A floral tribute to the princess from the frog: an old botanical print of a single red camellia, probably cut down years ago to fit into the 9 1/2 by 6 1/2-inch frame, $10, found on the top floor at Martha's Mixture, Richmond, Virginia. A closeup of the decorative details of the frame (also shown below and on page 223, number 4), once gilded, now reveals dusty old plaster where the gold has worn away.

Above: The romantic embellishments of View with a Room—the curlicue porch brackets, spindle railing trim, and shaped porch posts—once at home on the front porch of the Victorian farmhouse, seen below, were salvaged (thankfully) by my parents before its time had come. I wonder if the wee spirits seen at the front door came too? Hope so!

Right: A salvage yard still life of fluted columns and wrought-iron gate conjures up visions of ancient Grecian ruins at United House Wrecking, Stamford, Connecticut.

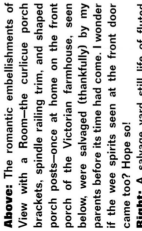

Above: The romantic embellishments of View with a Room—the curlicue porch brackets, spindle railing trim, and shaped porch posts—once at home on the front porch of the Victorian farmhouse, seen below, were salvaged (thankfully) by my parents before its time had come. I wonder if the wee spirits seen at the front door came too? Hope so!

Right: A salvage yard still life of fluted columns and wrought-iron gate conjures up visions of ancient Grecian ruins at United House Wrecking, Stamford, Connecticut.

to build a view

My View with a Room is a simply constructed 10 by 10-foot salt-treated pine platform. The 12-foot-long corner posts (4 by 4s) were sunk about a foot in the ground. The perimeter sill, about 3 feet off the ground, was created with 10-foot boards (2 by 6 inches). Six more 10-foot boards (2 by 6 inches) were secured with the perimeter square to support the 10-foot by 1-inch by 6-inch floorboards. The corner posts were further secured by a railing of boards (10 feet by 1 inch by 4 inches) at the top.

The idea here is not to build <u>my</u> platform (this is not an episode of "This Old House!"), but to create your own personal view of water, gardens, mountains, or woods. It could be as simple as a tent, a tepee, a gazebo crafted of wood and twigs or a driftwood tower if your view is of the ocean. Vita Sackville-West had a tower at Sissinghurst; Thoreau had his cabin on Walden Pond; I have my View with a Room. Each is a little altar to place ourselves on or in to commune with nature. Stake <u>your</u> claim.

1. Tubs to toy soldiers, nothing's off-limits on the grounds—30,000 square feet inside, and another 25,000 outside—of United House Wrecking in Stamford, Connecticut. On this particular visit I was on a hunt for old windows. Treasures found: four vintage Palladians, $100, and a dozen not-so-vintage four-paned sashes, $100. **2.** Though these fluted relics were spotted at United House Wrecking, salvage havens can be found in all regions of the United States. Check the Yellow Pages under "Antiques," "Architectural Salvage," "Building Materials," "Demolition," and "Salvage." **3.** If you are not as fortunate as I was in obtaining the architectural embellishments for my View with a Room, seen opposite, a set of four shaped porch posts similar to the ones seen here would cost you about $100 at Caravati's Inc., Richmond, Virginia.

TAG SALE: Fri./Sat., Dec. 13/14. Indoors. 62 Old Queechy Rd. Follow signs Rte. 295 after Canaan, N.Y. Market or Post Office intersection. Free gifts. Regulator clock, girl's bike, African sculptures, sterling flatware service, Modigliani drawing, luggage, mink collar, furniture, commemorative Wedgewood plates, small appliances, much more.

TAG Sale - Millerton, NY
Sept 4, 1995

junk guide

California

& etc.
1110 Mission Street
South Pasadena, CA 91030
(818) 799-6581
Thursday, 10:00 a.m.–4:00 p.m.
Friday and Saturday, 1:00–6:00 p.m.
Or by appointment

&
etc
antiques, art and etcetera
1110 Mission St., South Pasadena, CA 91030
(818) 799-6581   Herb & Yvonne Hazelton

Cleveland Wrecking
3170 East Washington Boulevard
Los Angeles, CA 90023
(213) 269-0633
Monday–Friday, 8:00 a.m.–5:00 p.m.
Saturday, 8:00 a.m.–1:00 p.m.

Krims Krams
3611 18th Street
San Francisco, CA 94110
(415) 626-1019
Monday–Friday, 1:00–6:00 p.m.
Saturday, 12:00–6:30 p.m.
Sunday, 12:00–6:00 p.m.

**Long Beach Outdoor Antiques and
Collectibles Market**
Veterans Memorial Stadium on Conant Street
between Lakewood and Clark Boulevards
Long Beach, CA 90808
(213) 655-5703
Third Sunday of every month, 6:30 a.m.–3:00 p.m.
Admission: $4.50

Pasadena City College Flea Market
1570 East Colorado Boulevard
Pasadena, CA 91106
(818) 585-7906
First Sunday of every month, 8:00 a.m.–3:00p.m.
Admission: free

Rose Bowl Flea Market
100 Rose Bowl Drive
Pasadena, CA
(213) 587-5100/(213) 588-4411
Second Sunday of every month, 9:00 a.m.–3:00 p.m.
Admission: $5.00

**Santa Monica Outdoor Antique
and Collectible Market**
South side of the Santa Monica Airport
on Airport Avenue off Bundy Avenue
Santa Monica, CA
(213) 933-2511
Fourth Sunday of every month,
6 a.m.–3:00 p.m.
Early admission: $5.00 before 8 a.m.

Urban Ore
1333 Sixth Street
Berkeley, CA 94710
(510) 235-0172
Monday–Sunday, 8:30 a.m.–5:00 p.m.

Colorado

Alderfer's Antiques
309 East Main Street
Aspen, CO 81611
(970) 925-5051
November 15–April 15 and June 5–September 15,
Tuesday–Saturday, 12:00–6:00 p.m.
Or by appointment

Trader's Way
17656 Highway 550
Montrose, CO 81401
(970) 249-3745
Open daily, 9:00 a.m.–5:00 p.m.

Three more great stops in Montrose, CO:
Triple D (970) 249-1954; A & A Antiques
(970) 240-8118; and Pattie's Antiques
(970) 240-9642

Connecticut

Doug's Used Furniture & Antiques
264 Kent Road
New Milford, CT 06776
(860) 355-2952
Tuesday–Sunday, 11:00 a.m.–5:00 p.m.

Elephant's Trunk Flea Market
Route 7
New Milford, CT 06776
(860) 355-1448
Sunday only, 7:00 a.m.–3:00 p.m.

Retro
266 Kent Road
New Milford, CT 06776
(860) 355-1975
Tuesday–Sunday, 11:00 a.m.–5:00 p.m.

Salisbury Antique Center
46 Library Street
Salisbury, CT 06068
(860) 435-0424
Monday–Sunday, 11:00 a.m.–5:00 p.m.
January–April, Friday–Sunday,
11:00 a.m.–5:00 p.m.

United House Wrecking, Inc.
535 Hope Street
Stamford, CT 06906
(203) 348-5371
Monday–Saturday, 9:30 a.m.–5:30 p.m.
Sunday, 12:00–5:00 p.m.

Villa's Auction Gallery
Route 7
Canaan, CT 06018
(860) 824-0848
Call ahead for hours

Florida

A–Z Swap
1697 Clearwater Largo Road
Clearwater, FL
(813) 586-5567
Monday–Friday, 10:00 a.m.–5:00 p.m.
Saturday, 10:00 a.m.–4:00 p.m.

The Banyan Tree
1775 Clearwater Largo Road
Largo, FL 34616
(813) 585-9462
Monday 12:00–5:00 p.m.
Tuesday and Wednesday, 10:00 a.m.–5:00 p.m.
Thursday–Saturday, 10:00 a.m.–6:00 p.m.

Country Village
11896 Wallsingham Road
Largo, FL 34616
(813) 397-2942
Tuesday–Saturday, 10:00 a.m.–4:30 p.m.
Sunday, 12:00–4:00 p.m.

Douglas Garden Thrift Shop
5713 N.W. 27th Avenue
Miami, FL 33142
(305) 635-6753
Monday–Saturday, 9:00 a.m.–5:00 p.m.
Sunday, 10:00 a.m.–5:00 p.m.

**Florida Victorian
Architectural Antiques**
112 West Georgia Avenue
Deland, FL 32724
(904) 734-9300
Monday–Saturday,
9:00 a.m.–5:00 p.m.

Fran's Treasure Trove
167-A Eglin Parkway
Cinco Bayou
Fort Walton Beach, FL 32548
(904) 243-3227
Monday–Saturday, 12:30–5:30 p.m.

The Hen Nest
5485 113th Street North
Seminole, FL 33772
(813) 398-1470
Monday–Friday, 10:00 a.m.–5:00 p.m.
Saturday, 10:00 a.m.–3:00 p.m.

J's Odds & Ends
11690 Walsingham Road
Largo, FL 34649
(813) 391-0789
Monday–Sunday,
11:00 a.m.–6:00 p.m.

50¢ EACH

ReTro
Antiques & Collectibles
Vintage Fabrics • Linens

home (203) 355-
-199

Bettina Calderone
266 Kent Rd. • New Milford, CT 06776 • 203-355-1975

**GIANT
TAG SALE
AT VILLA'S AUCTION GALLERY**
Route 7, Canaan, CT
**SATURDAY & SUNDAY
DECEMBER 14 & 15
10 am til 5 pm**

Partial List: Hundreds of items to choose from
including antiques, collectibles, used furniture,
household items, books, tons of glass & china,
plus much more! Also, a large selection of
beautiful bright handcrafted rocking zoo animals
(all brand new) great gifts for Christmas.

For more information: Call Richard Villa 860-824-0848.
We take cash, check, VISA & MC.

J'S ODDS & ENDS
FURNITURE, YARD TOOLS, BIKES, MISC
SALE
391-0789

231

NUSUAL ITEMS
STATE LIQUIDATION

ONE PIECE OR
ENTIRE HOUSEHOLD

KLUTTER KORNER
BUY - SELL - TRADE
Antiques-Furniture-Collectibles-Jewelry
Old Guns-Coins-Relics-Paintings
Household Goods-Tools-Primitives-Etc.

OL. JOE VARGO
HONE 813-734-2429

538 DOUGLAS AVE.
DUNEDIN, FL 34698

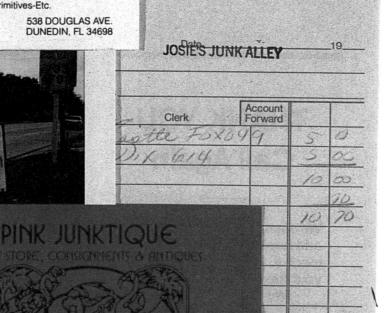

Florida (cont.)

**Josie's Junk Alley Thrift &
Consignment Store**
MM 99½
Key Largo, FL 33037
(305) 451-1995
Monday–Sunday, 10:00 a.m.–5:00 p.m.

Joyce's Thrift Shoppe
311 South Pinellas Avenue
Tarpon Springs, FL 34689
(813) 938-8190
Monday–Friday, 10:00 a.m.–5:00 p.m.
Saturday, 10:00a.m.–4:00 p.m.

Klutter Korner
538 Douglas Avenue
Dunedin, FL 34698
(813) 734-2429
Call ahead for hours

Little Ole' Lady Trading Post
314 Bayshore Drive
Niceville, FL 32578
(904) 678-7424
Monday–Saturday, 10:00 a.m.–5:00 p.m.

Pink Junktique
U.S. Highway 1, north, MM 99½
P.O. Box 3004
Key Largo, FL 33037
(305) 451-4347
Monday–Sunday, 10:00 a.m.–5:00 p.m.

Scavenger Hunt
3438 Clairmont Road
Atlanta, GA 30319
(404) 634-4948
Open daily,
10:00 a.m.–7:00 p.m.

Illinois

Betty's Resale Shop
3439 North Lincoln
Chicago, IL 60657
(312) 929-6143
Monday–Saturday,
9:00 a.m.–8:00 p.m.
Sunday, 10:00 a.m.–
8:00 p.m.

Salvage One
1524 South
Sangamon Street
Chicago, IL 60608
(312) 733-0098
Tuesday–Saturday,
10:00 a.m.–5:00 p.m.
Sunday, 11:00 a.m.–
4:00 p.m.

Kentucky

Smith & Hawken
Two Arbor Lane, Box 6900
Florence, KY 41022-6900
For mail order or a store near you,
call (800) 776-3336
http://www.smith-hawken.com

Maryland

Claiborne Ferry Furniture
10550 Miracle House Circle
Claiborne, MD 21624
(410) 745-5219
Call ahead for hours

Provence Art & Antiques
2620 Jewel Road
Belleair Bluffs, FL 33770
(813) 581-5754
Monday–Saturday, 10:00 a.m.–5:00 p.m.

Vanity Novelty Garden
919 4th Street
Miami, FL 33139
(305) 534-6115
By appointment only

We R Creative
394 Mary Esther Cutoff
Fort Walton Beach, FL 32548
(904) 863-3230
Call ahead for hours

Georgia

My Favorite Place
5596 Peachtree Industrial Blvd.
Chamblee, GA 30341
(770) 452-8397
Monday–Sunday, 10:00 a.m.–5:30 p.m.

Massachusetts

Brimfield Market
Route 20
Brimfield, MA 01010
(413) 245-7479
Open three times a year,
in May, July, and September,
6:00 a.m.–6:00 p.m. Call for specific dates.
Admission: $3.00; $7.95 for guide (three issues)

The Hadassah Bargain Spot
1123 Commonwealth Avenue
Newton, MA 12154
(617) 254-8300
Monday–Wednesday, 9:30 a.m.–5:30 p.m.
Thursday, 9:30 a.m.–7:30 p.m.
Friday, 9:30 a.m.–2:30 p.m.
Sunday, 12:00–5:00 p.m.

The Little Store
Route 7, north (just over the bridge)
Great Barrington, MA 01230
Closed in the winter
(No phone, no regular hours, but if you're
nearby, check it out!)

New York

Amenia Auction Gallery
Route 22
Amenia, NY 12501
(Closed temporarily, but if you're in the area,
give it a try!)

Antiques & Collectibles
Route 44
Washington Hollow, Salt Point, NY 12578
(914) 677-9922
Open most days until 5:00 p.m.

Alice Reid's Antiques in the Barn
P.O. Box 113
Livingston, NY 12541
(518) 851-9177
Call ahead for hours

**Alice Reid's at The Hudson
Antiques Center**
536 Warren Street
Hudson, NY 12534
(518) 828-9920
Call ahead for hours

New York [cont.]

The Ballroom Co-op
315 ½ North Franklin (upstairs)
Watkins Glen, NY
(607) 962-4473
Open daily, 9:00 a.m.–5:00 p.m.

Bottle Shop Antiques
Route 44
Washington Hollow, Salt Point, NY 12578
(914) 677-3638
Open daily, 11:00 a.m.–5:00 p.m., except Tuesdays

Anne Keefe Chamberlin
County Road 58, Coleman's Station
Millerton, NY 12546
(518) 789-3732
Saturday–Sunday, 11:00 a.m.–5:00 p.m.

Jack Christensen
Specializes in garden furniture and structures
625 Empire Road
Copake, NY 12516
(518) 329-4172
Call for information

Cindy's Antiques
P.O. Box 356, Route 22
Amenia, NY 12505
(914) 373-8851
Friday–Monday,
10:00 a.m.–5:00 p.m.

Collector's Corner
Northeast Center, on
Route 22, near Route 199
Millerton, NY 12546
Saturday–Sunday,
11:00 a.m.–5:00 p.m.

**Copake Country
Auction**
Box H, Old Route 22
Copake, NY 12516
(518) 329-1142
Monday–Friday,
8:00 a.m.–5:00 p.m.
Call ahead for auction times

Daisi-Hill Farm
RR 2, Box 370
Indian Lake Road
Millerton, NY 12546
(518) 789-3393
May 1–October 31,
Monday–Sunday,
10:00 a.m.–5:00 p.m.

Ed Herrington, Inc.
Patio stones and fencing
312 White Hill Lane
Hillsdale, NY 12529
(800) 543-1311
Monday–Friday, 7:00 a.m.–5:00 p.m.
Saturday, 7:00 a.m.–4:00 p.m.

Fort Brewster Trading Company
Route 22
Pawling, NY 12564
(914) 279-7460
Monday–Friday, 8:00 a.m.–7:00 p.m.
Saturday and Sunday, 8:00 a.m.–8:00 p.m.

The Garage Antiques & Collectibles
112 West 25th Street
New York, NY 10001
(212) 647-0707
Saturday and Sunday,
9:00 a.m.–9:00 p.m.

Hessney's Antique & Auction Company
405 Exchange Street
Geneva, NY 14456
(315) 789-9349 or (800) 924-9349
Monday–Saturday, 9:30 a.m.–5:00 p.m.

Hob Nail Antiques, Inc.
571 State Route 22
Pawling, NY 12564
(914) 855-1623
Monday–Sunday, 9:00 a.m.–5:00 p.m.

Howard Frisch
New and Antiquarian Books
Old Post Road
Livingston, NY 12541
(518) 851-7493
Friday–Sunday, 11:00 a.m.–4:00 p.m.

Johnson & Johnson Antiques
Box 361, Route 22, north
Millerton, NY 12546
(518) 789-3848
Friday–Sunday, 10:00 a.m.–5:00 p.m.

Madalin
55 Broadway
Tivoli, NY 12583
(914) 757-3634
Thursday–Sunday, 3:00–8:00 p.m.
Call for additional hours

MICHAEL FALLON
COPAKE COUNTRY AUCTION
Complete Auction Service
Box H • Copake, N.Y. 12516
(518-329-1142)

No. 2944

Lot # _____ MP - 3

_____ Gate

Millbrook Antiques Mall
Franklin Avenue
Millbrook, NY 12545
(914) 677-9311
Monday–Saturday,
11:00 a.m.–5:00 p.m.
Sunday,
12:00–5:00 p.m.

Maurice Neville, Jr.
Junk hauled by the truckload
RDF 3, Box 172
Camby Road
Millbrook, NY 12545
(914) 677-3687
Call ahead for information

Northeast Antiques
Route 22, near intersection with Route 44
Millerton, NY 12546
(518) 789-4014
Friday–Monday, 11:00 a.m.–5:00 p.m.

Potted Gardens
Flowers & Antiques
27 Bedford Street
New York, NY 10014
Tuesday–Sunday, 11:30 a.m.–7:00 p.m.

Potted Gardens

Rodgers Book Barn
467 Rodman Road
Hillsdale, NY 12529
(518) 325-3610
Monday, Thursday, and Friday, 12:00–6:00 p.m.
Saturday and Sunday, 10:00 a.m.–6:00 p.m.

Ruby Beets
Poxybogue Road and Route 27
Bridgehampton, NY 11932
(516) 537-2802
Friday–Monday, 11:00 a.m.–5:00 p.m.

The Rummage Shop
Route 22, north
Millerton, NY 12546
Sundays only, 11:00 a.m.–4 p.m.

Sage Street Antiques
Route 114 (Sage and Division Streets)
Sag Harbor, NY 11963
(516) 725-4036
Saturday, 11:00 a.m.–5:00 p.m.
Sunday, 1:00–5:00 p.m.

Second Chance
45 Main Street
Southampton, NY 11968
(516) 283-2988
Monday–Saturday,
10:00 a.m.–5:00 p.m.
Sunday, 12:00–5:00 p.m.

The Second Hand Shop
19 East Castle Street
Geneva, NY 14456
(315) 789-7504
Monday–Saturday,
9:00 a.m.–5:00 p.m.

Stan'z Used Items & Antiques
743 Ulster Avenue
Kingston, NY 12401
(914) 331-7579
Tuesday–Saturday, 11:00 a.m.–5:00 p.m.

Stormville Airport Antiques
Show & Flea Market
Route 216 (between Route 55 and Route 52)
Stormville, NY
(914) 221-6561
Call for dates

Tag Tale Antiques
Montauk Highway
Southampton, NY 11968
(516) 725-8157
Call ahead for hours

Terra Incognita Art & Antiques
47 Route 25A
Smithtown, NY 11787
(516) 366-3477
Call ahead for an appointment

Tomorrow's Treasures
Route 44
Pleasant Valley, NY 12569
(914) 635-8600/8402
Thursday–Sunday, 9:00 a.m.–5:00 p.m.

The Treasure Shop
92 Partition Street
Saugerties, NY 12477
(914) 247-0802
Monday and Thursday–Sunday,
11:00 a.m.–5:00 p.m.
Closed Tuesday and Wednesday

22 Junk-A-Tique
Route 22
Millerton, NY 12546
(518) 789-4718
Call ahead for hours

Twenty-sixth Street Flea Market
Sixth Avenue and 26th Street
New York, NY 10001
(212) 243-5343
Saturday and Sunday,
9:00 a.m.–9:00 p.m. year-round
Admission: $1.00

New York [cont.]

U-Name-It Shop
315 North Franklin Street
Watkins Glen, NY 14891
(607) 535-7565
Open daily, 9:00 a.m.–5:00 p.m.

Hard-to-Find ?
• Nippon, Crystal
• Depression Glass
• Roseville, Hull, Hall
• Appraisals, Estates
• 2500 Sq. Ft. Mall
• **NEW LOCATION**

Large Variety • Multi-Dealer Mall
919/441-9449 • Open Daily 7 Days a Week
½ Surfside Plaza (between highways) Nags Head, NC

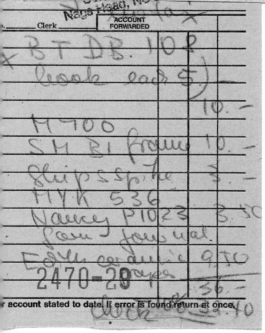

The Watnot Shop
525 Warren Street
Hudson, NY 12534
(518) 828-1081
Monday–Saturday, 10:00 a.m.–4:00 p.m.

Joseph Zullo
General Contractor
1200 County Route 27
Craryville, NY 12521
(518) 851-6935 (call after 6:00 p.m.)

North Carolina

Bermuda Triangle
Milepost 13½
Surfside Plaza
Nags Head, NC 27959
(919) 441-9449
Monday–Saturday,
10:00 a.m.–4:00 p.m.
Sunday, 1:00–5:00 p.m.

Hot Line Thrift Shop
Route 64
Manteo, NC 27954
(919) 473-3127
Monday–Saturday,
10:00 a.m.–5:00 p.m.

Hot Line, Too
Milepost 8½ on the Route
158 bypass
Kill Devil Hills, NC 27948
(919) 441-1244
Monday–Friday, 12:00–8 p.m.
Saturday, 12:00–4:00 p.m.

Kitty Hawk Building Supply
543 North Croatan
Kitty Hawk, NC 27949
(919) 261-2101
Monday–Friday, 7:00 a.m.–5:00 p.m.

Kitty Hawk Thrift, Consignment & Antiques
4622 Virginia Dare Trail
Kitty Hawk, NC 27949
(919) 255-0276
Open year-round. January–March:
Friday–Sunday, 10:00 a.m.–5:00 p.m.
April–January: Open daily 10:00 a.m.–4:00 p.m.

Merry-Go-Round Thrift Shop
Milepost 9
903 South Virginia Dare Trail
Kill Devil Hills, NC 27948
(919) 441-3241
Monday–Saturday, 10:00 a.m.–4:00 p.m.

A Penny Saved Thrift & Consignment Shop
3105 North Croatan Highway
Seagate North Shopping Center
Kill Devil Hills, NC 27948
(919) 441-8024
Monday–Saturday, 10:00 a.m.–5:00 p.m.

Pontes Antiques
c/o Twisted Fish
1903 South Croatan Highway
Kill Devil Hills, NC 27948
(919) 441-5757
Monday–Friday, 9:00 a.m.–5:00 p.m.
Saturday, 9:00 a.m.–6:00 p.m.

Charles Reber
Woodcarver
4600 South Roanoke Way
Nags Head, NC 27959
(919) 441-5307
By appointment only

Teen Challenge Thrift Store
Dare Center Mall
1740 Croatan Highway
Kill Devil Hills, NC 27948
(919) 441-1412
Monday–Saturday, 10:00 a.m.–5:00 p.m.

The Twila Zone
3330 South Virginia Dare Trail
Nags Head, NC 27959
(919) 480-0399
Monday–Saturday, 10:30 a.m.–5:00 p.m.

Texas

Room Service
4354 Lover's Lane
Dallas, TX 75225
(214) 369-7666
Monday–Friday, 10:00 a.m.–5:30 p.m.
Saturday, 10:00 a.m.–5:00 p.m.

Room Service Warehouse
1135 Dragon
Dallas, TX 75207
(214) 747-7666
Monday–Thursday, 9:00 a.m.–4:00 p.m.
Friday, 9:00 a.m.–12:00 p.m.

The Stardust
131 11th Street
Houston, TX 77009
(713) 868-1600
Saturday, 10:00 a.m.–5:00 p.m.
Sunday, 12:00 a.m.–5:00 p.m.

Tinhorn Trader
1608 South Congress Avenue
Austin, TX 78704
(512) 444-3644
Tuesday–Saturday, 10:30 a.m.–6:00 p.m.

Uncommon Objects
1512 South Congress Avenue
Austin, TX 78704
(512) 442-4000
Monday–Friday, 10:30 a.m.–6:00 p.m.
Saturday, 10:30 a.m.–8:00 p.m.
Sunday, 12:00 a.m.–5:00 p.m.

Virginia

American Junk
This is the flagship store of American Junk—just
opened in the spring of 1996. Y'all come!
489 Rappahannock Drive, P.O. Box 1094
White Stone, VA 22578
(804) 435-1840
Call ahead for days and hours

Buffalo Springs Herb Farm
Box 163, Raphine Road, Route 606
Raphine, VA
(703) 348-1083
April–December,
Wednesday–Saturday, 10:00 a.m.–5:00 p.m.

Caravati's Inc.
Restoration materials from old buildings
104 East 2nd Street
Richmond, VA 23224
(804) 232-4175
Monday–Friday, 8:30 a.m.–5:00 p.m.
Saturday, 9:00 a.m.–4:00 p.m.

The Twila Zone
Fine Vintage Clothing - Collectible
Antiques - Old Costume Jewelry
3330 S. Virginia Dare Trail   JoRuth Pa[...]
Nags Head, NC 27959   (919) 48[...]

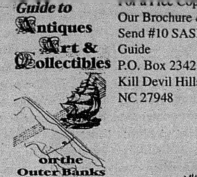

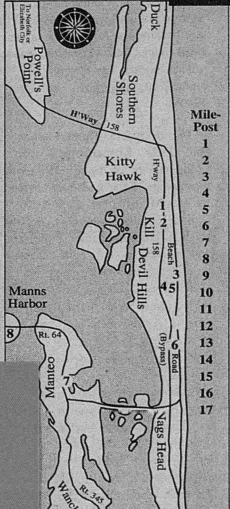

WELCOME TO THE HOME OF AMERICAN JUNK

hotline Thrift Shop
call Betty Butler

Virginia [cont.]

Cecil's Antiques
7 West Broad Street
Richmond, VA 23220
(804) 643-9273
Monday–Saturday, 9:30 a.m.–5:30 p.m.

D's Place
Holland's Stage Coach Markets
Route 17
Gloucester, VA 23061
(804) 693-3951
Saturday and Sunday, 10:00 a.m.–4:00 p.m.

Ikea Washington
Potomac Mills Mall
I-95, Exit 156
Woodbridge, VA
(703) 643-2687
Monday–Saturday, 10:00 a.m.–9:00 p.m.
Sunday, 11:00 a.m.–6:00 p.m.

Jim & Pat Carter's Real Estate
(If you decide to move to Virginia with
all your junk, call my father, mother,
or sister Emily!)
Box 7, Chesapeake Drive
White Stone, VA 22578
(804) 435-3001

K & W Antiques & Collectibles
Route 1, Box 2457
Route 200 at Rehoboth Church
Kilmarnock, VA 22482
(804) 435-0542 or (804) 580-7827
Thursday–Saturday, 8:00 a.m.–4:00 p.m.

King William Antiques and Refinishing
7880 Richmond Road
Toano, VA 23168
(757) 566-2270
Monday and Thursday–Saturday,
10:00 a.m.–5:00 p.m.
Sunday, 12:00–5:00 p.m.
Tuesday and Wednesday by chance

Lord Botetourt Antiques
6580 Main Street
Gloucester Court House, VA 23061
(804) 693-5402
Monday–Saturday, 10:00 a.m.–4:00 p.m.

Martha's Mixture
3445 West Cary Street
Richmond, VA 23221
(804) 358-5827
Monday–Saturday, 10:00 a.m.–5:00 p.m.

Pat's Attic Treasures
34 Chesapeake Drive
Route 200
White Stone, VA 22578
(804) 435-2499
Wednesday–Saturday, 9:00 a.m.–4:30 p.m.
Or by appointment

Penny Paid
Route 33, P.O. Box 26
Locust Hill, VA 23092
(804) 758-5280
Wednesday–Saturday, 10:30 a.m.–4:30 p.m.
Sunday, 12:00–4:30 p.m.

Stuckey's Antique Emporium
315 West Broad Street
Richmond, VA 23220
(804) 780-0850
Monday–Saturday, 10:00 a.m.–5:00 p.m.

Williamsburg Pottery
Route 60, west
Lightfoot, VA 23090
(757) 564-3326
Sunday–Friday, 8:00 a.m.–6:00 p.m.
Saturday, 8:00 a.m.–7:00 p.m.

Washington, D.C.

Georgetown Flea Market
Wisconsin Street between S and T Streets
Washington, D.C. 20037
(202) 223-0289
Sunday, March–December 25,
9:00 a.m.–5:00 p.m.

Wisconsin

Milwaukee Antiques Center
341 North Milwaukee Street
Milwaukee, WI 53202
(414) 276-0605
Monday–Saturday, 10:00 a.m.–5:00 p.m.
Sunday, 12:00 p.m.–5:00 p.m.

Rummage-O-Rama
Wisconsin State Fairgrounds
Exit 360 off I-94
Milwaukee, WI
(414) 521-2111
Call ahead for days and hours

Water Street Antiques
318 North Water Street
Milwaukee, WI 53202
(414) 278-7008
Monday–Saturday,
11:00 a.m.–5:00 p.m.
Sunday, 12:00–5:00 p.m.

Chair Ca

804-435-0542
804-580-7827

BASEMENT Clearance sale: everything must go, pool table, couch, furniture, clothes, misc. (413)-258-4087 for information.

JUNK

seed sampler

9 BORAGE

K & W —

...ques & Collectibles
...g & Furniture Refinishing

Rt. 1, Box 2547
Kilmarnock, Virginia 22482

PennySaver

USED ITEMS / NEW ITEMS

Antiques
JUN...

Newspapers, Directories, and Guides to Flea Markets, Auctions, Swaps, and Shops

American Junk Journal
Good gab about great junk—a junker's newsletter from yours truly! For information on it and other junker's stuff (like the bumper sticker shown on page 5) write c/o American Junk, RR 2, Box 118, Millerton, NY 12546

Antiques & The Arts Weekly
Bee Publishing Company
5 Church Hill Road
Newtown, CT 06470
(203) 426-3141
Weekly newspaper listing major antiques shows, auctions, and markets across the country, $48.00 per year

Clark's Flea Market U.S.A
419 Garcon Point Road
Milton, FL 32580
(904) 623-0794
A national directory of flea markets and swap meets, $8.50 per issue or $30.00 per year (4 issues)

Maine Antiques Digest
P.O. Box 1429
Waldoboro, ME 04572
(207) 832-4888
A monthly newspaper that lists flea markets in the U.S. and abroad, $37.00 for 12 issues

The Official Directory to U.S. Flea Markets
House of Collectibles
201 East 50th Street
New York, NY 10022
(212) 751-2600
A directory that provides essential information about flea markets nationwide, $6.99

SOUTHERN BERKSHIRE

SHOPPER's GUIDE INC.

Direct Mail

The Personal Medium

1968 ~ 1996
Celebrating our 28th Year Anniversary

35 Bridge St., P.O. Box 89, Gt. Barrington, Mass. 01230
Telephone (413) 528-0095 or 528-9094

Tri-State Circulation